VAMPIRISM

The hobo can't hear himself

think over the rattle and roar

of those trains he haunts

arms crossed and eyes closed

hanging in the cold dark like a bat.

The noise is as comforting to him

as that night he calls home

even in the daylight.

FAHRENHEIT 13

AN IMPRINT OF FAHREHEIT PRESS

RISING FROM THE ASHES OF THE MUCH LOVED NUMBER THIRTEEN PRESS - FAHRENHEIT 13 IS A NEW IMPRINT FROM PUNK NOIR VETERANS FAHRENHEIT PRESS.

NOIR LEGEND CHRIS BLACK IS INSTALLED AS EDITOR IN CHIEF AND IS ACCEPTING SUBMISSIONS NOW

F13NOIR@FAHRENHEIT-PRESS.COM

FAHRENHEIT 13 WILL RE-PUBLISHING ALL OF THE ORIGINAL NUMBER THIRTEEN PRESS NOVELLAS AS WELL AS COMMISSIONING AWESOME NEW CRIME FICTION FROM ALL AROUND THE WORLD.

PULP ★ CRIME ★ NOIR

WWW.FAHRENHEIT-PRESS.COM

@FAHRENHEITPRESS   @F13NOIR

CONTENTS

"If we don't believe in freedom of expression for people we despise, we don't believe in it at all."
--Noam Chomsky

Toxic Tribalism

The city of LA has fallen victim yet again to looting and rioting. The deafening rumble of helicopters scoured the city.
Stores were looted, a big rig ransacked at an intersection. Car windows were smashed with baseball bats. Two people were shot dead. All in one night. The usual suspects come to mind unemployment, civil unrest, the tyranny of the LAPD... Actually it wasn't any of those things.
The Dodgers won the World Series.
Imagine if they'd lost.

When you set foot into a foreign 'hood that's heavily involved, you'll be challenged.
"Where you from?" "What set you with?" All routine questions in gang occupied territory

If you never hear "So what's up?" you've got a better than average chance of surviving the challenge. Being involved. Being with someone has its advantages. There's strength in numbers. If you don't know, it all boils down to red or blue. Rattling off the name of your 'hood, or who you roll with are acceptable answers, along with the one I always use: "I don't bang."

That identifies me as a civilian. An independent. Unfortunately in today's socio-political climate, there is no equivalent. If you don't pick an ideology, you're going to be assigned to one. It all boils down to red or blue. Strength in numbers. But it's more than that. It's about righteousness. Being on the righteous side. The side that supports freedom of choice. Unless you disagree with one or two points, and find out you're just wrong. That's when you find out what it's all about. Power. The mob rules. And these days they're ruthless. But it isn't the other mob they're attacking. It's the individual who doesn't bang. The mob recently came after me. (we had a difference of opinion). I was labeled a red sympathizer. I understand how important it is. To be involved. To be accepted by advertisers. But try and understand, I don't bang. And I don't roll with the Demicrips, or the Rebloodlicans. And let me ask you this...Since you want to pigeon hole me. Does it make sense for a bootstraps guy like me to align myself with a duplicitous oligarch? If you want to ride the current indefinitely, you'll eventually have to change directions. And if your mob loses its power, believe me when I tell you, those individuals you swarm attacked have a long memory. And you might just feel the slightest tinge of regret...

Meeting that individual by chance in an alleyway without the mob at your back. Or maybe not. It's not too late to bring back 'live and let live', and respect everyone's freedom of choice on every single issue. You know who else loves cancelling people? Donald Trump.

Dave Chappelle, *Sticks and Stones*. Bill Burr's monologue on SNL—these are your wakeup calls. I look around and see people who ride along just to impose their will. There are cops like that. Real liberalism is to protect and allow freedom of choice. The mob always rules. But no one mob rules for long.
Be good to each other.

——Scotch Rutherford, Managing Editor

"A GENRE-DEFYING VAMPIRE FILM"
Patrick Frater, VARIETY

BLOOD *from* STONE

a GEOFF RYAN *film*

starring

VANJA KAPETANOVIC   GABRIELLA TOTH   NIKA KHITROVA   ERIC COTTI

GEOFF BLACK   NIKA KHITROVA   ALETHEA SPENCER   ADESHOLA ADISUN   SARAH MCLUSKY   STEVEN YAP

LINDA NELSON   MICHAEL MADISON   GEOFF RYAN   MICHAEL CARADONNA   GEOFF RYAN

INDIE
REJECTS
MOVIES

ACTION
on
CAMERA

NOIR HAYES
RAZOR BLADES
ENTER THE MINDS OF THE MOST
DANGEROUS GANGS IN THE CITY.

SAINT CATASTROPHE

SARAH JILEK

rk, trippy, and exquisitely visceral. If Flannery O'Connor's and Daniel Woodrell's
ional worlds collided, Jilek's writing would be their wild and precocious literary
e child." —LAURA BENEDICT, Edgar-nominated author of *The Stranger Inside*

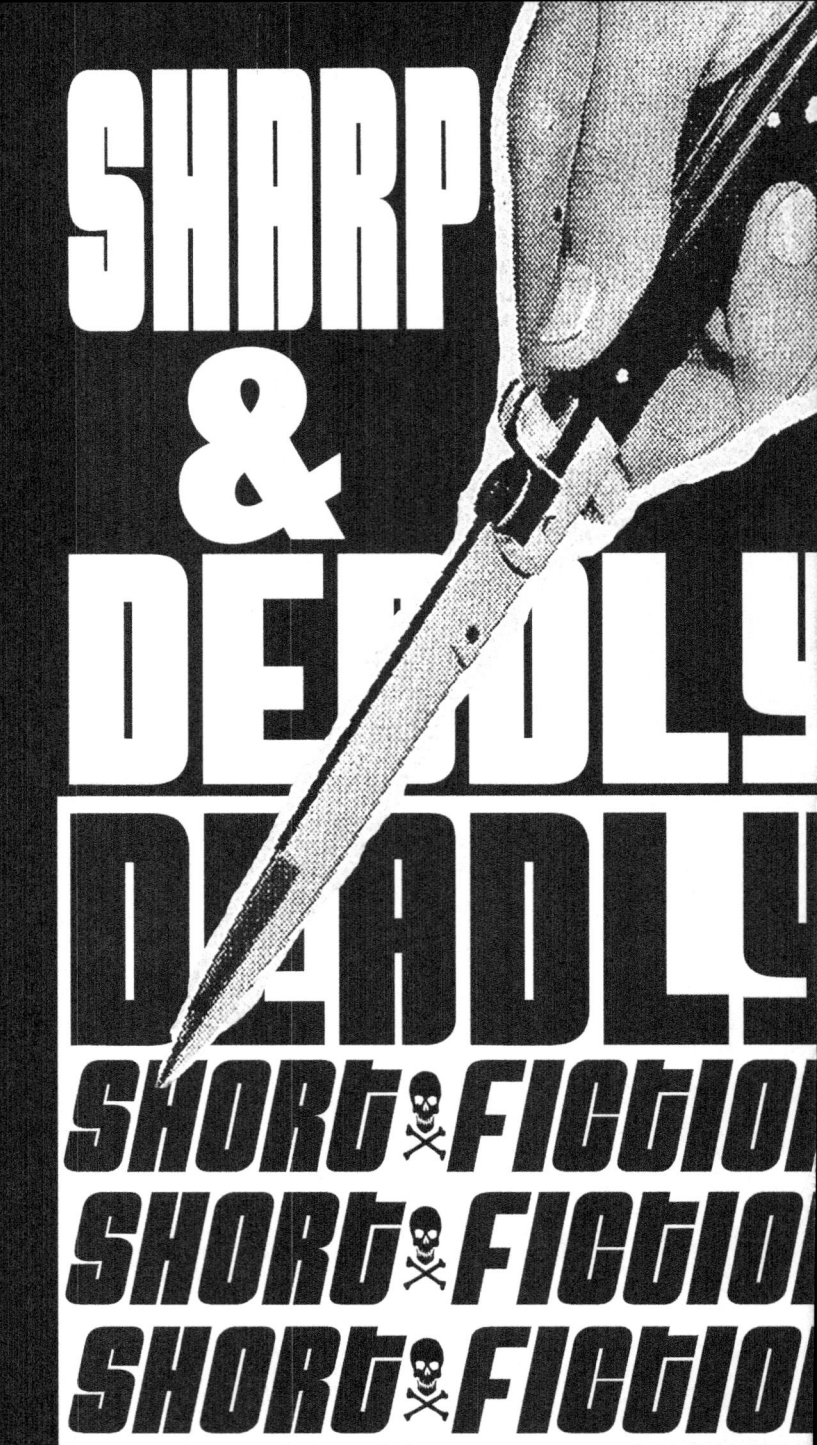

The blood washed off, though, in a way, the red stain remained. Pulling a tooth chip out from between his knuckles, Detective Simmons considered the jaw his hammer hands opened. Wide enough for a confession to drool out, he deemed that reason to be proud. Another case closed by the crimson badge, he dropped the chip and listened to it clatter down the drain.

Hands aching, he left the precinct to grab a quick bit of peace and quiet. No one inside seemed sorry to see him go. The crooks for obvious reasons, while the other cops got a little less subtle each day about their desire to see Simmons catch a bullet. So, he vanished to his usual sleep spot.

Most folks didn't care for the yoga strain of sleeping like a "Z" in cramped theater seats. Having done it since childhood, escaping to the screens when Pops got to swinging an empty bottle, Roland Simmons enjoyed napping in the cinema. Although, the Admiral Theater didn't feature what some snobs considered *cinema*. Skin flicks sneered at because they lacked pretentious dialogue.

Tonight, the silver screen offered little lullaby. Funk bass and fake orgasms beating eyes open. The leading lady in this picture hammed it up with moans that wouldn't fool a virgin. Her shrill phony screams shattered any chance of proper slumber. Vodka more than anything else put Simmons to sleep. Yet, though the sandman arrived, little time passed before the detective stirred. Simmons grumbled, reluctantly returning to the waking world.

Stretching, bones audibly popping back into place, Simmons glanced around. Judging by the ladies making their way along the aisles it must've been after sundown. The late show side hustle featured a bevy of hookers happy to help give any onscreen scene a little tactile reality. So long as no one got to straight up screwing in the aisles, management let the lite jobs slide. Some degree of decency needed to be maintained. Even if it only amounted to an illusion.

Shush-rip. Simmons glanced toward the sound. He saw a stick figure drifting toward him. Feet sticking to the floor, *shrip-shrip* with every step.

"Not interested," Simmons said.

"Maybe I just wanted a seat," she replied flopping down, a space between them. "It's easier to be left alone where it's lonely."

"Uh huh," Simmons said.

"I'm Ivy," she said.

"Don't care."

"Solo artist," she said. "I can respect that, but if you'd like an audience, it'll only cost a dollar."

Simmons started fishing in his pockets. It took a minute, but he eventually found his badge. Flashing it at the hooker, he expected her to vanish like a vampire confronting a cross. Disappearing in an explosion of pleather bats and needle scabs. Instead she smirked.

"So, am I a double D-tective in this scenario?" she said. "Show me your evidence partner."

Simmons leaned closer, "This is real, not a joke."

"And you're not the first cheap cop to expect a freebie."

Simmons got up. He knew a losing situation and preferred not to bother. It was always easier to walk away.

Out in the lobby he went straight to bathroom. Backed up toilets turned the interior into an urban wetland. Ceramic tiles spongy underfoot. Once yellow, the brown tint to them felt more familiar. Disgustingly reassuring due to their constancy. Not much lasted in this city, but the Admiral's tiles remained unabashedly filthy.

Walking over to the farthest stall, Simmons yawned. A sign hung crooked declaring the toilet out of order. Ignoring it, Simmons went inside. Opening the toilet tank, he found the inside bone dry. Good thing considering the contents deposited earlier.

From within he fetched a small bottle of mouthwash, a plastic pint of vodka, and his gun. Swishing mouthwash, he holstered his gun. Spitting in the toilet he returned the mouthwash, exchanging it for a bottle of pills. Simmons shook out two of the *ya ba* inside, a Thai concoction mixing methamphetamine with caffeine. Washing them down with a shot of vodka, Simmons always thought that amounted to adding gasoline to jet fuel, but he couldn't argue with the results. Everything except the gun back in the tank, he exited the stall.

Ivy stood leaning against the sink.

"This is the men's room," Simmons said.

"Oh, my bad," Ivy rolled her eyes. "I've never been in one of these before."

He gave her a quick scan. She dressed like a country girl. Triple-X parody, obviously, but the act's intention came across clear. Her pigtails played at being a teenager, though her eyes spoke of a hard road to thirty.

"I heard you playing the maracas," she winked. "You need clean piss? I know some kids over on Seton Street that'll fill a bottle."

"You mean the runaways in that shit hotel?" Simmons scoffed. "I'd rather squeeze a dog dry."

10

"I bet you would."

Something in the way she regarded him made Simmons nervous. She looked hopeful. So, he again exited quickly.

He pushed out onto the street. Two seconds later, Ivy popped up alongside him.

"Are you like an actual decent cop?" she asked.

"Who hangs out in porno theaters?" he countered, worried where this might go.

"Yeah, but most people mind their own business in there," she said.

He frowned. There's nothing worse than an insightful hooker. They've seen too much to be lied to and been beaten too many times for a harsh word to send them running. Only the truth would set him free.

"Fine," Simmons said. "If you want, you can call me decent. So what?"

"I need help."

He figured a pimp needed a beating. Her makeup hid the wreckage well, but detective eyes saw through the veil. A simple curb stomp should suffice, and truth be told, he'd enjoy the task. Then she spilled the beans making a whole mess of the evening.

*

There's a stretch of downtown called Meat Street. Piss, blood, vomit, and rain keep the asphalt shiny and slick. Pedestrian piranhas pound the pavement looking for anything to eat. The ground glitters thanks to the specks from a thousand broken bottles. One for every dream shattered along the avenue. Dull eyed prostitutes line the boulevard, while pimps strut about singing like peacock carnival barkers.

"Street buffet, street buffet, screw however you want today."

Simmons lit a cigarette. He blew out through his nose, canceling the odor of this rotting meat locker. Ivy sparked a gasper as well, a hand rolled beauty. Simmons did his best to ignore the marijuana aroma. Mostly because it made his mouth water.

"That's him," Ivy pointed at a wood paneled station wagon.

Amidst the usual slow flow, Simmons spotted the vehicle. It looked ten years overdue for a trip to the junkyard.

"Got it," Simmon said. "Wait here."

He stepped into the street. He maneuvered easily between the traffic. Cars here always cruised molasses slow, though the station wagon crept along even slower. Slow enough for Simmons to cross the street and hop in the passenger seat.

The driver almost jumped out. Simmons grabbed him by the collar. He grimaced, feeling its dampness.

"Don't hurt me," the driver said. "I'm just looking."

"You looking for something in particular?" Simmons said.

The driver hesitated. It took all of two seconds for the cop to clock a suburbanite out of his depth. The realities of the city too jagged for him to handle with those soft suburban hands. His greatest problems probably amounted to existential dilemmas not fighting off a crackhead ready to knife for a pair of shoes.

"Pull over," Simmons said holding up his badge.

The driver promptly parked. Simmons asked for a name.

"Wallace Tanner," the driver said.

"Okay, Wally, here's the deal," Simmons said flicking ash across the dashboard. "You're making some of the ladies around here nervous. Seems you tried to snatch one the other day."

"I thought I found her," Wallace said softly.

"Don't interrupt," Simmons snapped. "See, these folks don't normally go to the cops officially which means I'm here unofficially which means I can do a lot of bad things. To you. Understand?"

Wallace nodded. Simmons pinned the smoldering coffin nail between his lips then suddenly slammed Wallace's face into the steering wheel. Once, twice, holding him down on the third.

Wallace squirmed but one hand held him down. The guy looked like a flock of birds could carry him away. Meanwhile, Simmons ripped open one pant pocket then another until he found Wallace's wallet.

"Go home," Simmons said, letting him loose as he took the cash and driver's license from the wallet.

Wallace sat up. His nose looked dented but not broken. Eyes cast down he didn't move, just sat there bleeding, red dripping off his chin onto his khaki's.

"But I haven't found her," Wallace said.

"You aren't gonna find Mrs. Right down here, buddy."

Simmons spotted a fortune cookie in the cup holder. The *ya ba* always made him snacky, so he snatched the cookie for later.

"You got it wrong," tears started dripping out of Wallace's eyes. "I'm looking for my daughter."

13

A part of Simmons said to just walk away —
not your problem— but with the *ya ba* kicking in, a
downside to meth is it makes everything feel
possible.

"What's she look like?" Simmons asked.

Sniffling, Wallace rolled up a flannel shirt
sleeve. On his forearm, a mediocre portrait of a
grinning little girl made Simmons queasy. She
didn't look older than ten or twelve.

"This is the only picture I have of her," Wallace
sighed. "That's why I made a mistake. I thought I
found her and just needed to take my sweet,
sweet Kasey home."

Wallace stroked the face inked into his arm.

"Fair enough," Simmons said, opening the car
door he hesitated. "If you think you see her again,
give me a call. Don't be snatching no ladies. Got
it?"

He handed Wallace a card. Without looking at
him, Wallace took it. Getting out, Simmons
slapped the roof of the station wagon, signaling
Wallace to take off. The car shuddered down the
boulevard.

Simmons went back to Ivy. She stood chatting
with a tall transvestite in a blue latex dress. He
caught the edge of their conversation. Gutter
glamor Barbie and cross-dresser Ken exchanging
fashion tips. However, Ivy stood with her back to
him. For the first time, Simmons spotted a raven
tattooed on her exposed lower back. That meant
Ivy belonged to Madame Raven. It struck him as
odd given her birds didn't usually need outside
help.

Knowing a cop on sight, the transvestite
departed — "See you around Ivy. I'll take care of
that polish."

"Paint it black," Ivy said cheerily.

14

"So, I talked to him," Simmons said. "I don't think he'll be back around."

"And if he is?"

He handed her his card. She tucked it in her shoe.

"I guess that's it then," Ivy said. "Unless you'd care for a special thank you?"

Simmons turned and walked away. He wandered the streets until familiar neon called him inside. A pleasantly doughy bartender, curvy and soft, armed him against sobriety, and Simmons fought reality one sip at a time.

"Hard night Simmy?" Kinga, the bartender, asked.

"They're all hard," Simmons said. "But I've seen worse."

Later, shooting his third shotgun shell of Russian water, the phone rang. Dancing, badly, around a pool table, Simmons knew by the ring's tone — the call came for him. He waved to the bartender.

"I got it Kinga," he said.

She shrugged and went back to pacing idly. Simmons came around the bar. The phone practically jumped off as it rang. Catching it mid-holler, he answered.

"What do you need?"

"Simmons, finally," the gruff voice of detective Holland answered. "I called three dives before I fucking found you."

"That's because you're not a good cop," Simmons replied lighting a smoke. "What's up?"

"Homicide. You really need to be in on this."

"No, I don't," Simmons considered hanging up; however, making three calls was a lot of effort for someone like Holland. "Where at?"

"Alley off the Meat Street. Between the China food place and that sad kiddie care for hookers' kids."

Simmons felt a knot twist in his gut. He waved to Kinga, a gesture requesting she refill his shot. She went right to it, pouring as she carried him a fresh artillery shell.

"What does she look like?" Simmons asked as he accepted the triple. "I'm guessing some sorta country girl?"

"Not even close," Holland said. "Some guy with your card on him."

Simmons felt relieved. Instead of firing his shot, he sipped it slow. He first guessed Ivy ran into some trouble with a pimp, some greasy pile of shit and fists who didn't like seeing her with a cop. Simmons didn't mind being wrong, at least not under these circumstances.

"I'll swing by," Simmons said, hanging up before Holland replied. "I'm taking this to go."

"Whatever," Kinga shrugged.

She fetched a red plastic cup from under the bar, a privilege afforded certain regulars. Simmons dumped his vodka in the cup then walked out. Red in hand, he tried not to think where this night seemed to be taking him.

*

Simmons approached the alley sipping the last of his cup. Some gawkers clogged the entrance but no one he couldn't shove aside. He tossed the empty over his shoulder before ducking under yellow tape. A rookie beat cop tried to stop him. Simmons used his badge to shoo the kid away.

Holland stood at the side entrance to the Chinese restaurant. Chomping on an eggroll, he spoke with his mouth full while questioning a collection of employees gathered in the doorway.

16

A young lady in a cheongsam stood at the front of the group. The mandarin gown hugged her as if it'd been painted on. She translated for Holland, though Simmons wondered how honestly she shared. The raven on her wrist suggesting some degree of duplicity.

Seeing Simmons, detective Holland waved.

"What's the situation?" Simmons asked.

Holland pointed to a nearby dumpster. Glancing over, Simmons saw a photographer snap a pic. The flashbulb lit the whole alley for a tick. Just enough time to glimpse the starburst of blood splashed across one wall. Streetlights knifed deep into the dark alley, but only enough to illuminate a pair of sneakers peeking out from behind the dumpster.

Holland scratched his beard, knocking out bits of eggroll. He ordered the restaurant staff to stay put, leering at the hostess as he backpedaled toward Simmons. Already on his way to the corpse, Simmons didn't need to ask. Holland offered up the details.

"That childcare center phoned it in," he said. "Thought some asshole tranny was blasting fireworks in the alley. Beat cops came, found this."

Coming around the dumpster revealed a flannel shirt and khakis adorning a body with half a head. It didn't take a genius to guess some of the moist bits dotting the ground weren't discarded meat from the Chinese restaurant.

"Because of the pockets," Holland said pointing at the torn pants. "We figured a robbery until we found your card in the shirt pocket."

"Then you figured a robbery that needed to stay quiet."

"That's what the blue wall is for," Holland said. "I know you forget that, but I doubt you're one to go around blowing open heads with a shotgun."

Holland reached into a pocket. Using a penlight, he lit the bloody wall. A peppering of dark holes pocked the old brick.

"Who's this guy?" Holland asked.

Simmons handed over Wallace's license. Then he filled Holland in on the details. According to Ivy, before becoming a corpse Wallace cruised Meat Street looking for his daughter. Thinking he found the young lady, or at least someone who looked close enough, he tried to drive off with a hooker, who panicked, rightly so, because who knew what kind of brainwashing bunker lay in store as Wallace reprogrammed her to be his lost child. In any event, she managed to get away. Enter Ivy, a friend of the almost abducted, who dragged Simmons into the affair.

"You think some pissed off meat dealer did this?" Holland said.

"That'd make sense," Simmons said, though something felt off.

He glanced around the alley. Graffiti on one wall, black feathers adrift, connected dots like the hostess's tattoo. This territory belonged to Madame Raven. No one careful would kill here without permission, and she rarely hid her executions. She preferred public displays; bodies hung from traffic lights.

Fishing for cigarettes, Simmons felt a plastic wrapper. Pulling out a fortune cookie, he decided to chat with the hostess.

"Can I get some fortune cookies?" he asked.

She snapped the order and a busboy soon returned with a handful. Plucking one, Simmons

18

compared the packages. They matched, a red *Fú* printed on both wrappers.

"When's the last time he was here?" Simmons asked.

The hostess shrugged.

"Fine," Simmons shook his head. "We'll do this the hard way. Is she here? And don't pretend you don't know who I mean."

The hostess hesitated. Simmons pushed his way inside. A waiter tried to grab his arm. He grabbed the young man by the balls, squeezing to pop them, and pushing back until the screaming waiter spilled backwards across the kitchen floor. Stepping over the groaning body, Simmons made his way into the restaurant.

Oblivious to the awfulness in the alley diners quietly ate while an erhu, pipa, and piano filled the room with soft music. Bursting from the kitchen like a hobo leaping off a train, Simmons scanned the room. In a dark corner he saw a statuesque African American woman sitting alone. Simmons didn't figure the mountains flanking her table counted as dinner company.

He went straight towards her. The mountains stirred. Simmons raised his hands.

"Not here to cause trouble," Simmons said. "Just got one or two questions."

Madame Raven eyed him. He felt the dagger in her eye slice him open, vivisect and assess him. She gestured and the mountains parted. Simmons took a seat across from her.

"I assume this is about the mess in my alley," she said.

He watched her use lacquered chopsticks to pick at steamed chicken and black mushrooms. Her own private pair not the disposable splinters on every table. Watching her delicately dine, he

19

considered her reputation, the corpses she caused. Meat sacks full of powdered bone, snitches devoured by sewer rats, and the numerous bloated totems hung over intersections, bodies even the cops ignored for a few hours, giving the message time to spread. Simmons knew he needed to choose his words carefully.

"Your alley, but I get the feeling it isn't your mess," he said.

That raised an eyebrow. Raven dabbed at her mouth with a napkin.

"What makes you say that?" she asked setting her chopsticks aside.

"I know this guy tried to snatch a working girl the other day," Simmons said. "If she was one of yours we'd've found this idiot impaled on a fire hydrant."

She held up a teacup. A waiter promptly refilled it.

"Go on," she said.

"But I know he ate here."

"I don't know all my customers."

"I don't expect you to," Simmons said. "Still, he didn't come here by accident. The guy's looking for his daughter, and he already thinks she's on Meat Street; well, if it's me, I'm going to ask the main vendors, ya follow?"

"And if he came, perhaps I heard about his inquiries?" Madame Raven said.

"Or dealt with him directly. Can't expect a distraught dad to do things the right way."

"Not like a boozy cop," Madame Raven remarked.

Simmons chuckled. Bits of her origin flashed to mind. Left for dead in a Triad brothel, she slaughtered her way up from reluctant hooker to *hóng táo huánghòu*, a remorseless queen of

20

hearts chopping off any head that opposed her. She eventually took over the Triad's old headquarters, this restaurant, a symbol of her empire's ascension. The detective knew even a toe over the line risked getting chopped off.

"I'm looking for the exit," Simmons said. "I just think you can point me the way."

"Since you're on your way out," Madame Raven said as she resumed eating. "I had no answers for him or his terrible tattoo. He seemed to think a child doesn't grow after fifteen years. So, I made him leave. What happened next is your riddle to unravel."

*

Simmons returned to the alley. Hooking up with Holland, the detectives decided to visit the childcare joint next door. Simmons hung back, while Holland took the lead, asking the lady in charge routine questions.

Wandering around, Simmons saw a little boy drawing with crayons. The picture wouldn't win any awards, though its content came across clear. It showed an adult man in a purple suit getting shot full of holes. The little person on the page doing the drilling bore a resemblance to the young boy. However, the purple suit certainly suggested Tony Buddha Blaze, a meat dealer with a mean reputation.

"You see that happen?" Simmons asked.

"No," he said. "It's what's going to happen."

Simmons nodded. He knew this place stood closer to a farm than a childcare center. Parents, about to work on Meat Street, planted their kids here. Then the next generation of hookers, hitmen, and worse blossomed. No pressure from proprietors like Madame Raven, let the world warp the children. They just stood back and

21

harvested whatever grew. Though, a few roses occasionally bloomed among the weeds.

About to say something to the kid, Simmons heard Holland call his name. Turning he saw the detective waving him over. Simmons left the boy behind. When he got near, Holland filled him in.

"I was asking if Deborah recognized our victim."

Deborah, the lady in charge, stood regarding Wallace's license. Her yellow dress implied a sunniness her face tried to deny, a cheek slit into a perpetual Cheshire frown. She chewed her thumbnail while eying Wallace's photo.

"I feel weird," Deborah said.

"Why's that?" Simmons asked.

"This guy," she said returning the ID. "Now that I know who it was, I don't feel bad that he's dead."

Holland cocked an eyebrow. Neither needed to ask for her to elaborate. Deborah told them that a few nights back, Wallace, though she didn't know his name then, shuffled inside. Playing with some kids, Deborah didn't notice him until Marcy started screaming.

"Who's Marcy?" Simmons asked.

Deborah pointed to a little girl sitting alone in a corner. She sat reading to a stuffed bunny. Something about her face poked at Simmons like a needle.

"She's seven," Deborah said. "He grabbed her like he was hugging her. Tight. Marcy started screaming then he tried to carry her out."

"What happened then?" Holland asked.

"I managed to cut him off before he ran out the door, but I had to rip her out of his arms."

"Is she okay?" Simmons asked, nodding towards Marcy.

22

"She was spooked a bit," Deborah said. "But these kids see a lot. She'll be fine."

"He say anything?" Holland asked. "Why he wanted her?"

"He showed me some bad tattoo on his arm," Deborah said. "Tried to insist she was his daughter."

"Could she be?" Holland asked.

"No," Deborah shook her head. "I know her parents. Her mother and I used to work together until…"

She trailed off, gesturing at her face. The prominent scar full of implications neither detective felt a need to explore. However, Simmons noticed black feathers tattooed, encircling her wrist.

No surprise this place belonged to Madame Raven. Granted, she didn't invent the concept of childcare for hookers' kids. Some slick pimp back in the day figured that one out. Seems the ladies worked harder knowing their kids were safe, and depending on one's degree of evil, the children inside could be insurance that a meat dealer's supplies didn't run off. That said, it inspired a question.

"What did Madame Raven say when you told her?" Simmons asked.

Deborah shook her head. She started chewing her nail again. Simmons figured she might gnaw it clean off one day.

"So, you didn't tell her?" Simmons said.

"Marcy's mom asked me not to," Deborah said. "She said she'd tell Madame Raven. I don't like being responsible for, ya know, what happens."

The conversation then circled back to why Deborah described the shooter as a transvestite.

23

While hanging some of the kids' art in the front window, adorable cutesy content not the warning signs of burgeoning psychopaths, she recognized the person heading into the alley.

"I've seen her around," Deborah said. "Don't know her name, but that blue dress is hard to forget."

That rang a bell. Furrowing his brow, Simmons glanced over at Marcy. He imagined her with pigtails, and it all made sense.

*

Ivy stood on a street corner sucking down a pint. She half-heartedly called out to passing prospects. Simmons watched for a long while before approaching. She saw him coming and spread a crooked grin.

"Howdy, decent cop," she said, tossing the empty bottle away. "Care to buy me another whiskey?"

"That depends," Simmons said. "Is it for Ivy or Kasey Tanner?"

"Kasey's dead," Ivy smirked. "Fell in the gutter grinder a long time ago."

Simmons didn't need much to guess at the story. He heard it too often in every variation. Dark days at home pushing her out the house, runaway or throwaway—it didn't matter. Out the frying pan into a black hole.

"So, Wallace is your father," Simmons said.

Ivy nodded. She mentioned avoiding him on Meat Street. Simple enough, since he kept looking for a little girl not a grown woman. Mad daddy never possessed a solid grip on reality. Then he heard about Raven's Chinese restaurant. From there Wallace stumbled on the childcare center.

"Thought she was me," Ivy said. "Crazy fuck tried to snatch my Marcy. Momma bear ain't having that."

So, Ivy called in the claws.

"He had a choice," Ivy spat. "I got you first, telling him to leave but told my gallows gal, if you see him around the daycare shoot my daddy in the face."

Ivy swayed like a ship lost at sea. She couldn't tell Madame Raven. The Madame's solutions meant paying a price.

"They'd want Marcy," Ivy said. "I've seen it before."

Simmons didn't need to hear anymore. Putting an arm around Ivy, he half carried her to Kinga's bar. There he deposited her in a booth where she promptly curled up and fell asleep.

Ordering a triple, Simmons got on the phone.

"Holland?" Simmons said. "I got word from an informant Tony Buddha Blaze is who you're looking for. Bring him in. He'll deny it at first but." —he flexed his hand, readying the hammer— "I'm sure I can get him to talk."

Hanging up, he drained the shot. It went down like a burning sermon. Leaving Ivy in Kinga's capable care, Simmons headed out to put a deserving sinner between the hammer and the anvil.

***

FRANK VINCENT
KATHRINE NARDUCCI
MIKE STARR
WITH STACY KEACH
AND ARMAND ASSANTE
CHICAGO OVERCOAT
"FANS OF THE FUNERAL AND THE BOONDOCK SAINTS WILL EAT THIS UP"
- CHICAGOIST
"THE MOST CHARISMATIC MAFIA MURDERER SINCE TONY SOPRANO"
- VARIETY
THE GLORY DAYS ARE BACK

BROWNSVILLE

GENE BREAZNELL

inner city schoolyard
bleak, abandoned
down a dead-end street
dull concrete walls
faded graffiti
rusted chain-link fence
two young lovers toss an old tennis ball
she in yellow, he in black
the ball slips through a hole in the fence
rolls toward an open storm drain
she takes chase, trying to save it
he just stands there, laughing like a fool

Sally chased her dreams all the way to LA, got a part in a movie. I stayed in Brooklyn, got ten-to-fifteen for grand theft auto. Fuck that bitch. Not Sally. The judge who sent me up for so many years. Sally sent me a postcard in prison with a photo of the famous Hollywood sign. 'Hooray for Holly-would!' she wrote on the other side. I didn't know what she meant by the mis-spelling. It was all she wrote, with no return address. I knew what that meant. Fuck me.

I got paroled after seven for good behavior, because they never found out who shivved Rico in the showers. And because of my poem about the schoolyard. The parole board thought it meant I recognized the error of my ways and was a changed man. Yeah, right. I had simply jotted on a scrap of wastepaper what happened that day between Sally and me. The board helped me get a job back in Brooklyn, where it happened. Not the executive position I thought I deserved, with a six-figure salary, corner office, unlimited expense account, secretary with deep cleavage. Also no company car. But the job did involve cars, at a full-service car wash. What better line of work for a car thief? More deep thinking by the powers that be.

On Rockaway Avenue in Brownsville, the poorest section of Brooklyn, with the highest violent crime rate, the car wash was owned and run by a guy everyone called Big Abe. Built like a bull walrus, Big Abe had a similar disposition. Always throwing his weight around, bellowing orders, growling his displeasure, with a stogie clenched between tobacco stained tusks. My job was spraying mud and road salt off wheels and out of wheel wells with a high-pressure hose before the cars went through a tunnel with automatic sprayers and scrubbers to wash the bodies. The hours were long, the pay minimum wage, with no sick days and no medical benefits. But lunch was free at *Chick-fil-A,* only on Sundays.

Full service meant dashboards got wiped, ashtrays emptied, carpets vacuumed, glass Windex-ed. Customers waited for their cars outside at the end of the tunnel. Among a dozen or so employees, I was the only one Big Abe didn't trust to clean the car interiors. Considering GPSs in glove boxes, Ray-Bans in consoles, loose change in cupholders, I didn't blame him. My first week, however, we were short handed. Big Abe was away, the guy he left in charge let me vacuum carpets, and I found a gun under the front seat of a Jetta.

*

Three blocks west of Rockaway Avenue and the car wash, deeper in the heart of urban darkness, I rented a studio apartment in a tenement that should have been condemned. The fourth-floor walkup came furnished with a squeaky bed, shaky table, rickety chair, no AC or TV. The mini-fridge was mildewed, the stove had only one working burner, the plumbing fixtures leaked. The warden, I mean slumlord, said he would get everything fixed, and get rid of the cockroaches. I didn't believe him, but couldn't afford anything better. I hid the gun behind the grate for a heating vent. Risking another ten-to-fifteen years upstate, no parole this time. It seems unfair when convicted felons need home protection like everyone else. But why worry? The little old lady driving the Jetta could not have known the .38 snub-nose revolver was under her front seat. Someone else must have put it there. She wouldn't know which end of a gun to hold. If she did know, so what? Finders keepers.

*

My first week at the car wash, the first week in August, the weather was hot, mist from the sprayers cool, business brisk. So brisk there was little time to talk with fellow employees and get to know them. No time to talk with customers. Not with Big Abe watching us like a prison guard. While car after car marched single in an endless file past my spray station. Like days in a poem Sally could recite from memory. Each day brought diadems and fagots, offering choices. Choices too often ignored, before the days turn and depart silent, and it's too late. Sally chose to follow her dreams, heading for Hollywood. I chose to stay in Brownsville, boosting BMWs.

My job spraying wheel wells, like making license plates upstate, was mindless, repetitive. Dull and unimaginative were the car models and colors, so many SUVs, almost all either black, white or gray. The occasional red, blue or whatever color did nothing to break the monotony six days a week, weekends and holidays with no time off for good behavior. Apparently no one told Big Abe that Abe Lincoln freed the slaves.

*

Big Abe has an office of sorts. More like a storage room, with towels, soap, hoses, nozzles and such. Now it's the last day of August. He calls me into his office, closes the door so we're alone, and says with big fat grin, "Had enough?"

"Am I getting fired?" I hope not. Not yet anyway.

31

"I've got another job for you," Big Abe tells me. "Do it right, it means a promotion and an increase in pay."

"No more spraying wheel wells, like a stray dog lifts its mangy leg?" I toss out, trying to be funny, hoping he doesn't take it the wrong way.

He laughs, so his belly rolls. "It's right up your alley," he says. "Grand theft auto, right?"

I nod. It's no secret.

"One count?"

Another nod.

"One got you sent up," he says. "But before you got caught, there must have been others."

No nod this time. Do I trust this guy? He drives a Lincoln. Everyone calls it Abe's Lincoln. But no one calls *him* Honest Abe.

Shifting his stogie from one corner of his mouth to the other, he says, "Never mind, kid." He always calls me kid. I don't think he remembers my name. "I don't care how many cars you stole."

"Then what's that got to do with anything?" I ask.

"I need you to steal a car for me," he says. Like saying go to the corner store and buy me a loaf of bread.

"Whoa!" I hold up both hands like a traffic cop. "I'm not going back to prison."

"Relax, kid." He laughs again, his belly rolls like before. "It's not stealing. It's a prank. My wife's car. I want you to hide it for me. Teach her a lesson she'll never forget."

"Hide it? Where?"

"I'll let you know. Don't you forget you're an ex-con. I did you a favor by hiring you. Now I need you to return the favor. Now get back to work."

Something doesn't sound right but that's all he'll tell me. It bothers me the rest of the day. By quitting time, however, I finally decide it must be a harmless prank. I'm okay with pranks as long as they're harmless.

Trudging back to my apartment after work, legs stiff from standing up all day, back sore from bending into wheel wells, I stop in at a corner bar for a cold beer. I've stopped here several times before. Talked baseball with the bartender. Told him I work at Big Abe's car wash. Now he hands me a longneck Bud and says the guy sitting next to me at the bar also worked for Big Abe.

"No more," says the guy, tells me his name is Rollo. He likes to talk. "Worked for that prick over a year. Worst year of my life but I never complained, always showed up on time, worked hard, never asked for a day off the whole year except one. Guess which one."

Instead of a guess, I hazard a shrug. I don't feel like talking, or hearing Rollo's life story, but there's no stopping him.

"Martin Luther King's birthday," he says. "And you know what he told me?"

Another shrug. I'm no mindreader.

"No way. But he told me I could take Jefferson Davis's birthday off instead of MLK's. Ain't that some shit. Shoulda busted his lip."

The bartender laughs, buys him a drink.

"So I waited," Rollo continues. "Jefferson Davis's birthday rolled around and I took the day off without tellin' the fat prick. Next day I showed up for work on time as usual. But he was all kinds of pissed. I reminded him about what he said but he fired me anyway."

There's a lesson here. But after two more beers, or is it three, I forget it.

*

At work the next day, Big Abe calls me into his office again. "Tonight at nine," he says, tossing me a car key. "My wife's Cadillac will be parked out in front of our house in the street. Drive it to this address." He jots an address and the code to a keypad on a scrap of paper, hands it over. "It's a warehouse. Know where it is?"

"I know the street." It's in the Red Hook section. Near the container terminal for ocean freight, servicing Brooklyn's only remaining port. Used occasionally for illegal drugs coming into the country, stolen cars going out.

"Thought you would," he snickers.

"You shipping the car overseas?" I ask.

"Never mind," he growls. "Drive it inside the warehouse, leave the key in a

34

cupholder on the center console, wait outside for me. You'll need a ride back."

*

Big Abe's house, on Howard Avenue, is in a fairly safe neighborhood for Brownsville. Easy walking distance from my apartment, the house is modest and middle class. But compared to my tenement it's the Taj Mahal. His wife's Cadillac, big, black, shiny, new, is parked in front of the house like he said. Climbing in behind the steering wheel, before starting the engine I need to familiarize myself with the instruments. Trying to figure out how to turn on the headlights and take off the parking brake. It's been awhile since I last drove a car of any kind. Seven years in fact. During which time my license expired. I forgot to tell Big Abe and he didn't ask. But Red Hook is not that far from Brownsville. What can go wrong?

I like this Caddy. It drives like a dream. The stereo is heavenly. The leather seats make me feel like a king. And the gas tank is full. I should just keep going, forget Big Abe, and follow my dreams. Like Sally. The Verrazano Bridge to Staten Island is only a stone's throw away. From there it's a hop and a skip to New Jersey, and a lope down the Eastern Seaboard to Miami on cruise control. I read somewhere that every shit-wad in the country shows up in South Florida at some time or other. So why not me?

I'm not going back to prison, that's why.

Headed west on Eastern Parkway traffic is light all the way to Prospect Park and Grand Army Plaza. Traffic on Union Street is lighter still. Unusual even for this time of night, Brooklyn being New York City's most populous borough. Where did everyone go? Except when passing through Park Slope, where my ritzy ride lets me blend, I feel like a fish out of water.

Red Hook is on a peninsula in southwest Brooklyn that bleeds into New York Bay. The view of Manhattan's skyline across the bay is inspiring, glittering like the Milky Way. The view down the dead end street near the container terminal where Big Abe has sent me is grim. There's nothing but warehouses, dark and deserted, with bars on the windows. There are no other cars. The only streetlight, dim as a D-student, makes the Caddy look blacker than black. Like the lead car in a funeral procession. Or like the hearse. And now it hits me. Stopping under the streetlight, I pop the Caddy's trunk, get out and look inside. In time see two cars turn onto the dead end street, tires screeching, light bars flashing. I know why they're here and who sent them. I don't need to find the warehouse anymore. I need the gun from the Jetta, the little snub-nose revolver that kindly came loaded with all six rounds. Lucky I brought it along. But I only need one round. I'm not going back to prison.

***

DEBT COLLECTORS

David Harry Moss

LIQUOR

DELI

What started as a typical day, a "business as usual" day, for Nick Hardin and Louie Grillo, leg breakers for a Brooklyn loan-shark, took an unexpected and terrible wrong turn. Three were dead, a cop lay on the street bleeding from a severe head wound, and police sirens were closing in.

Nick was twenty-nine, 6'5" and a solid 270. He sparred with boxers in the toughest New York City gyms and knew enough combat sambo to make him a vicious street fighter. Louie, a six feet two-inch, 325-pound wrecking ball, was nine years older than Nick, and an ex-pro wrestler. Nick wore jeans, a black T, dark blue hooded sweatshirt, and steel tipped shoes, good for cracking bones. Louie wore tent-like cargo khakis, sturdy walking shoes, a loose fitting, blue shirt, and a brown windbreaker.

It began at 7:30 A.M. in a crowded gab and eat diner where Nick and Louie were wolfing down pancakes, scrambled eggs, and sausage. Nick's cell phone rang.

Vince Rubino, the guy Nick and Louie worked for, said in his guttural voice, "Where the fuck are younze guys?"

Nick grinned. "In a house of prayer."

"Fuck you, Nick. Where?"

"We're in Red Hook. Planning our day."

"I hope your fucking planning includes making some collections."

"We got the paper in front of us."

A sheet of paper with a list of "must sees", "welchers on loans", rested on the table between the platters of food.

Vince worked out of a little office in the Rubino Fish Market in Bensonhurst. "I'd like to see some fucking dough on my desk before the little bit of hair I have left on my head falls out."

"You should give up this stressful line of work, Vince."

"I'm thinking about it. In the meantime, where's your first stop?"

"Brownsville, and the switchblade knife man, Randolph Sparkle."

Nick did the driving, a big green Grand Marquis with tinted windows.

Nick nibbled on his lower lip. "Maybe I should check on my squeeze first. When I left her last night, she was coming down with something."

Nick's squeeze was a six-foot-tall, dark haired beauty, a fetish model and actress in erotic flicks, named Elena Garko.

"Before we do that, stop at a street vendor. I'm in the mood for some shredded cabbage and maybe a tamale."

Nick pulled the car behind a street vendor's cart so Louie could get his cabbage and tamale.

With Louie hogging down the cabbage and tamale, Nick drove in the rain on traffic clogged Van Brunt for several minutes before cutting through Gowanus and entering Park Slope.

Nick pulled onto an east to west side street of elegant Brownstones built at the turn of the last century and parked the car under a line of trees in a tow- away zone. He put a phony "New York City Building Inspector" sign on the dash. Rain kept falling. Water dripped from the trees and puddled on the sidewalk. Two pretty females holding hands under an umbrella strolled by. "Girls in love, how romantic," Nick mused.

Nick swung out of the car. He had a key to get into the front door of one of the Brownstones but no key to get into the building itself. A tenant had to buzz him in. He hit the buzzer for Elena Garko.

While he waited, Louie chugged prune juice from a quart bottle.

Several minutes later Nick returned to the car. "She's fine. She's on her cardio treadmill bare ass naked: and I left her to be here with you."

"You're breaking my heart."

Fifteen minutes into what should be at most a thirty-minute ride from Park Slope to the *Randolph Sparkle Car Wash* on Pitkin Avenue in Brownsville and they were gridlocked in east Brooklyn heavy traffic. An abandoned apartment building had caught on fire and sirens and fire trucks were coming from all directions. The rain had stopped leaving the air muggy.

"It's ten o'clock already," Louie said. "Fooling around with your babe messed up our whole day."

Nick scowled. "I was with her for five fucking minutes."

"More like twenty-five and me waiting for you messed up my system. Suddenly I got to take a shit," Louie added.

Nick wasn't surprised. Mixing prune juice with a ton of food. "Hold it."

"Yeah sure," Louie growled. "That's easy for you to say."

Nick grinned and tapped the steering wheel with his knuckles. On the sidewalk people, mostly black or Hispanic, one interested Nick, a hot-looking, caramel-colored girl in a mini, strolled by. "Who was tougher, Bruno or Killer Kowalski?"

"Who cares?" Louie muttered. "I got to take a shit bad, remember." Even though the windows were down and damp air blew into the car Louie sweated as if he were in a sauna. He wiped his balding head with a white towel, squeezed his big ass cheeks tightly, and squirmed in the seat.

Amused, Nick's grin broadened. With buzz-cut black hair, a strong jaw, straight nose, a slight thin scar on his left cheek, and a swarthy complexion, Nick, a Russian-Ukrainian mix, was good-looking in a roughhewn way. Women found Nick intriguing; men were wary of him. "What about Rik Flair? Or Hulk Hogan?"

"Them guys was before my time and fuck them anyway."

"In a real fight, against someone like me, how would they do?"

"Screw that already," Louie snarled. "The pressing issue isn't if them guys were tough, or if them guys could take you, it's me having an attack of the runs coming on."

Nick smiled. "That's what you get for hogging down all of that food. You never have any self-control when it comes to eating."

"Skip the Little Odessa wisdom and get me to a fucking commode before I defecate myself," Louie snarled.

Suddenly, Nick made a sharp right turn the wrong way into a one-way alley. "There's a fag joint at the end of this alley," Nick said. "You can shit your brains out in their john."

"How do you know about places like that?"

"Elena had this bit part as a bounty hunter in a crime movie, and they shot a scene in there."

Louie grinded his big ass into the seat. "Let me out. I'm about to unload."

Nick's smile broadened as he hit the brakes and Louie lurched forward. "Go through the rainbow-colored door by that dumpster," Nick said. "It should be unlocked for the cleaning guy. The shitter is on the right."

Before Louie could fling open the door a police car, red dome light flashing, pulled up behind them. Nick peered into the rearview and frowned. Louie squirmed, made a labored breathing noise and grunted, "Great. I'm ready to explode and a badge shows."

A well-built blond-haired cop, Nick's age, got out of the police car and swaggered up to the Grand Marquis.

Nick knew the drill. He rolled the window down and handed the cop his driver's license and owner's card. Nick said, "My buddy has to take a shit. While you're writing me up any chance of him getting out of the car and going into that bar?"

The cop sized Nick and Louie up and down and his narrowed brow and twisted lips said he didn't like what he saw. He squared his shoulders and his scowl darkened. "Either one of you dick heads get out of this car unless I tell you to and you both get maced, understand?"

Nick shrugged, nodded, leered, and muttered, "Thanks."

"This is an emergency, bro," Louie pleaded. He tried to make his voice soft and congenial but failed. There was too much gravel in it.

"Shut up, fuck-off." The cop spoke in harsh insulting tone to provoke Louie who managed to stay calm.

43

This cop was gung-ho and on some kind of a mission, Nick reasoned.

Louie scowled and lowered his eyes while Nick looked the cop over. The cop was in short sleeves and what stood out was his eighteen-inch arms. Nick looked at Louie and said, "Biff Biceps doesn't like us much."

Chewing on his lower lip, Louie stared straight ahead. "Maybe an enema would settle him down. A good cleansing shit works wonders."

The blond-haired cop took his time writing the tickets. When finished he shoved the papers at Nick and said, "This is for illegally going down a one-way street and for neither one of you goombah scumbags using seat belts. Any questions or arguments go to the 73rd precinct and complain. My name is on the ticket. Sean Crone."

Nick shook his head. "No questions or arguments at all officer Crone. Have a lousy day."

As the cop pulled away Louie snapped, "Asshole."

"He called us goombah scumbags," Nick muttered.

"Say what?"

"I got a feeling we're not done with that cop. I got bad vibes about him and got this image in my mind of us coming at him with guns in our hands."

Louie rolled out of the car, took two quick steps, and stopped. Looking at Nick through crestfallen eyes he said, "I didn't make it."

Nick shook his head in mock sympathy. The seat of Louie's pants was suddenly brown and sopping wet. "Go inside anyway and wipe your ass. And throw your shorts away. You can't sit in this car drenched in shit."

Louie glared down the alley in the direction the cop, Sean Crone, had gone and screamed, "I'll kill you, you cock-sucker."

Nick drew his lips back in a rueful smile and said, "Don't say cock sucker inside. Someone might take you up on it."

Thirty minutes later Louie got back into the Grand Marquis. He sat on the towel. "I mean it, Nick, I'm gonna whack that dirtbag cop. Trust me. I'm gonna put a slug right between his fucking eyes."

Nick rolled the window down more letting in gas-fume laced air. "I don't know what smells worse," Nick said to Louie, "you or the smog."

Quivering with rage, Louie said, "Take me home so I can clean up."

"Take you home. We're five minutes from *Randolph Sparkle's Car Wash*."

"I don't give a fuck if we're in the parking lot. I can't be seen, or smelled, in public like this. It's humiliating."

Nick backtracked and twenty-five minutes later, after passing Grillo's Pizzeria, owned by Louie, pulled in front of the brownstone in Carroll Gardens that Louie owned also and where he lived.

No rain fell but the sky remained swollen and had darkened even more. None the less, Nick slipped on a pair of sunglasses. "Hurry up, okay. It's eleven thirty already and we got people to see." Nick switched off the ignition and shut his eyes. Behind the dark lenses of the sunglasses he felt secure thinking that no one passing by, an enemy possibly, could see him resting his glims.

45

Louie hurried inside carrying the towel he'd been sitting on. Nick got a picture of Louie arguing with his wife, a spunky Italian about his weight, while taking a shower. She probably jammed into the shower stall with him and kept hounding him as he dressed in clean underwear and trousers.

Louie had four kids, two boys, two girls, ages three to thirteen, fatsos like Louie and his wife, and maybe one or all of them were in the house piling on him about how heavy he was. Nick didn't regret not being married. He lived alone, did what he wanted to do with no static, and liked it that way.

While he waited for Louie to shower and change clothes Nick got two phone calls. The call from a fighter at Gleason's Gym who needed a sparring partner he didn't answer. The call from Vince he did.

"Did you get around to getting any of my fucking money?"

"Not yet."

"Whatta you mean, not yet?"

"Louie had a little accident that derailed us."

"What kind of a little accident?"

"He shit himself."

"Maybe I should just replace you two jabronis with somebody else."

Nick's jaw muscles stiffened. His lips tightened. "Go on Vince," Nick snapped, "replace us if you got somebody better."

Nick could hear the sound of Vince tapping something against something metal. Nick guessed the something metal to be the hubcap sized ashtray loaded with cigar butts on his desk and the tapping instrument to be a

46

set of brass knuckles Vince used as a paper weight and intimidator.

"That's the fucking trouble," Vince grumbled, "there is nobody better at this kind of business than you and Louie. You guys could scare Frankenstein."

"Then relax. We'll have some dough for you by the end of the day."

Nick shrugged Vince off and envisioned Elena looking so yummy on that treadmill. He saw succulent tits bouncing, long legs flowing, firm lovely ass cheeks gliding, and the moist lips of a shaved pussy quivering. Blood rushed into his loins.

Just as Nick started to get hard, Louie emerged wearing clean baggy brown khaki pants, a clean white shirt, sneakers, and the windbreaker. Nick shrugged. He removed the sunglasses and started the car.

Louie got back into the Grand Marquis reeking of musk-scented cologne.

"What took you so long?" Nick pulled out into traffic.

"I needed to give my wife time to tell me how much she worries about my health and how I should quit the rackets and concentrate on that pizza shop we own and maybe open another one."

"Sounds like a good plan." Nick was in the process of acquiring a business of his own, a little fitness center that catered to women in Bay Ridge where he lived. If it worked out, he'd put his leg breaking days in the rear view.

"I'm pissed. Nick. Like I told you, I'm gonna whack that muscle-bound fucking jack-off cop. Blast his fucking head off."

Nick narrowed his eyes and tightened his lips. "Biff Biceps?"

"Yeah. Biff the prick Biceps."

"Do what you have to do," Nick said, rolling the window down all the way again to rid the car of the repugnant cologne smell. "What did you douse yourself with, skunk piss?"

"I got another bottle of it in the house. I'll give it to you."

"Don't do me any favors."

Finally, at two o'clock, Nick and Louie were sitting in the waiting room of *Randolph Sparkle's Car Wash* in Brownsville where they had just collected ten grand on a five-thousand-dollar loan. Vince's interest rate on this loan was a hefty 100%. The room smelled of cigarillo smoke and Lysol.

Randolph stood in front of them, staring with sinister eyes, shuffling his feet, toying with a bright ring on his well-manicured pinky finger.

"Tell Vincent I'm truly sorry he had to send you gentlemen," said Randolph, a knife blade thin, slope shouldered, silver haired black man and the owner of the car wash. Randolph wore a light blue pinstripe suit and purple tie. He had the mellow voice and the slick, elegant persona of a seasoned conman.

"You'd be a lot truly sorrier if you didn't have the dough," Nick said, sullen faced. "We like you Randolph but not that much."

"I know that, Nick-o-las. I know. But if you don't mind my saying, it does seem unfair that Vincent charges that exorbitant interest." Randolph lit a thin brown cigarillo.

"I do mind you saying and who forced you to borrow from Vince?"

48

Randolph's lips twitched. "No one did, Nick-o-las. But I had nowhere else to turn." He dragged on the cigarillo.

"There's banks."

Randolph blew out a thoughtful column of smoke. "I walk into a bank, even walk past one, and the alarms go off."

"Then be glad that Vince is there for you. Be more careful with your dough and you won't need a loan shark. I got no sympathy for you or anyone else who deals with Vince."

Randolph's eyes dropped to the floor. "I see your point."

"In the meantime, scour the front seat on the passenger side real good," Nick said. "Real extra good."

Randolph shifted the thin stub of a burning cigarillo across his thin lips and said, "Will do, Nick-o-las. How did the seat get so soiled?"

Nick said, "Louie shit his pants," and Randolph snickered

"He's fucking joking," Louie said through a mouthful of a bean and cheese burrito he was munching on. Louie had purchased the burrito in the Hispanic fast food restaurant next door. "Some coffee got spilled."

Across the street a cop car pulled behind a gunmetal gray van with rust and dents on the fenders. The van with fumes spewing from the exhaust was parked in front of a liquor store. A big blond-haired cop got out.

Nick nudged Louie. "Louie, there's your pal, Sean Crone."

"I don't know no Sean Crone."

"Biff Biceps."

Louie looked out the window, glowered, but kept eating.

As Sean Crone swaggered toward the driver's side of the van the front door of the van flew open. A tall dude wearing a red Satan mask jumped out.

"Oh my," Randolph said. The corners of his lips pulled. "Oh my."

Both Nick and Louie caught on too and sprang to their feet. Before the cop could react two other men, both wearing red Satan masks, exited the liquor store. The taller man of the two packing a sawed-off shotgun, and shorter man, carrying a handgun, hurried around from the back of the van.

As the cop turned the taller man cracked the cop on the skull with the handle of his shotgun. The cop teetered. One of the other men said something to the cop who abruptly dropped to his knees and clasped his hands behind his bleeding head, execution style.

"They're going to kill that cop," Randolph bleated, "they're hopped up on some bad shit and they are going to kill that cop right there on the street in front of my carwash and I'm not seeing it. No sir, I'm no witness for that fucking action."

Nick looked at Louie, calmly shrugged his shoulders, and said, "Your call."

"My call for what?"

"Do we get involved? Do we let them kill that prick or do we step in and try to stop it?"

"What are we, do gooders, guardian angels?"

"You decide."

Louie said, "Everything tells me no, we stay here, let the lousy prick die."

Nick shrugged. "If that's how you want it."

The tall dude with the sawed-off shotgun had it pressed to the back of the cop's head. At any moment he could pull the trigger.

Louie sighed. "I can't let it happen," Louie grumbled. "I want to, but I can't. If I did my Mother", he crossed himself, "and my Father too," he crossed himself again, "would come out of the ground after me for sure."

Nick nodded. "I kind of knew it would play like this. You're a lot of things, Luigi," Nick always called Louie that, "most not so good, but heartless slob isn't one of them."

Louie and Nick rushed through the door. Once on the street Louie took a final bite from the burrito and tossed it away. With compact .45 automatics pressed against their sides, they strode across the street, nearly getting hit by a fast-moving pickup truck, the driver, oblivious to what was going on, blaring the horn and giving them the finger.

Smiling grimly in the direction of the van, Nick said, "Hi guys, nice masks. Need some help? Is everything all right here?"

As the taller man snapped, "Fuck you," and swung toward Nick and Louie with the sawed-off shotgun Louie got off three shots. One bullet struck the gunman in the chest; the other bullets took out a window in the van. The frightened cop hit the concrete face first as the shotgun discharged and the roar of pellets blasted a hole in the street sending chips of concrete flying into the gunman's face.

Nick fired six of the eight rounds in his clip; Louie fired the five left in his,

most of them hitting the van. The shorter man's face exploded a moment after he got off a wild shot that struck a parked car. The third man;

he raised his gun but too slowly and didn't manage to pull the trigger, dropped into a puddle of blood, thrashed violently, and then as if asleep, stopped moving. Louie aimed his empty gun at the cop's forehead. "Get up, you scumbag."

The cop, shaking with the fear of death, pushed himself to his feet. He said, "They were going to kill me." He tottered side to side. A wet stain front and back showed on his trousers.

From nearby, mixing with the fading echo of the gunfire, approaching police sirens wailed. The fouled air now burned of gunpowder. Vehicle traffic had stopped, and gawkers crowded the sidewalks. A roly poly black guy standing by the van and staring mortified at the dead bodies started babbling in ghetto slang and waving his arms hysterically.

Louie smiled. He said to the cop, "I see you shit your pants." He lowered his gun, let his right arm hang at his side.

"Yeah, I did." With the back of a hand the cop wiped at the blood flowing over his face from the wound on his skull.

"Pissed them too," Louie said. "You're a fucking mess. Couldn't happen to a bigger prick." Louie slipped his gun into a shoulder holster strapped against his white shirt. "Do you remember me?"

"Yeah. You and your partner, you guys just saved my life."

Nick shoved his gun into its hip holster under his hoodie. "When the goon squad arrives, we'll be in the car wash across the street."

"I owe you guys everything," Sean Crone blurted. Blood covered his face. His hands wouldn't stop shaking. "You saved my life. I came this close," he parted his fingers an eighth of an inch, "of being dead."

"All you owe me is to lose, or pay, those traffic tickets you gave us and one carwash," Nick said.

"And you owe me a new $100 pair of pants, size 48 – 33, a pair of boxer shorts, as large as they make them, and a burrito," Louie sneered. "Then I hope I never fucking see you alive again."

Crossing the street Nick said, "You never paid a hundred bucks for a pair of pants in your life, you cheap prick."

Louie grinned slyly.

When they reached the other side of the street Louie veered toward the fast food Hispanic restaurant. "You want something, Nick?"

Nick shrugged. "Sure. One of them burritos."

Nick and Louie wasted two hours waiting in *Randolph's Car Wash* while the cops verified their CCW, concealed carry weapon gun permits, and did their crime scene work outside.

At least they kept the TV news people away. All the cops gave out was that two good Samaritans saved a police officer's life. Throughout the ordeal, uniformed NYC cops trooped into Randolph's Carwash with praise and congratulations.

"Can't you do this someplace else?" Randolph asked, chewing on a cheroot. He kept blinking his eyes, shuffling his feet, and rubbing his sweating palms.

Nick grinned. "What's wrong, Randolph?"

Randolph said, "You know what's wrong. I'm up to my false choppers in stolen property. There's enough goodies stashed in the back

53

room, flat screen TV's mostly, to put me away for ten years."

Louie smiled mischievously. "Maybe we should turn you in and really make points with the law." When Louie saw Randolph cringe Louie said, "Just messing with you."

A quartet of homicide detectives came in to shake Nick's hand and Louie's hand. "We have respect for the law," Louie told them. "We admire cops."

Nick sat back and closed his eyes. When his cell phone rang, he answered it, listened to Vince rant, and said, "You found out about the little incident we had in Brownsville fast, Vince."

"Little," Vince snorted. "It's all over the fucking news. Three members of a satanic kill cult shot dead. A cop wounded and almost executed. You'd have to be living in a fucking cave in the Himalayas not to hear about it."

"How'd you connect it to me and Louie? Our names weren't mentioned. The TV cameras never caught us."

"When I heard *Randolph Sparkle's Car Wash*, I knew," Vince bellowed. "Who else but you two would have the balls to go up against psycho members of a fucking satanic cult armed with sawed-off shotguns? It's unbelievable. Nick Hardin and Louie Grillo working with the NYPD. This world gets more fucked up every day."

"You done Vince? There's a slew of news reporters heading this way."

"Whatever ever you do, don't mention my name and keep those fucking guns in their fucking holsters. You're debt collectors not fucking hit men. We don't kill people; we just scare them. Break bones if need be. This is a fucking civilized operation I run. Capice."

When the scene finally had cleared, while heading for the car, Louie said to Nick, "You feel like another one of them burritos?"

"Yeah, sure."

The sky had almost blackened; and hard lines of rain began to fall.

***

©2020 David Harry Moss

‹EXIT

THE EVOLUTIONARY PURPOSE OF CARING

STANTON MCCAFFERY

When she walked into my office at the middle school, I knew in an instant who she had been. I had no idea, however, who she was.

Allow me to clarify.

Cynthia Smith had been a student of mine. It was early in my teaching career. She was still young, younger than you would expect for the parent of a middle schooler. And I was old. At least I felt old. I felt decades and decades older than I had been when I knew Cynthia and engaged in the act I imagined she remembered me for.

Her son was at the school for a week before he disappeared. I had only heard about him from the guidance office. Before his mother came in with her makeup tear-streaked down her face, I hadn't thought much of his disappearance. It wasn't that I didn't care. It was that we deal so often with homeless kids. They come to school for a week and that's all we see of them. They relocate. With no word from anyone, we assumed that's what happened with Henry, Cynthia's son.

Now, I mentioned caring there; how I cared about the kids even if I didn't know their stories or worry too much when they suddenly left the school. I have to say a few things about that right at the beginning of this story.

You always care. Nobody goes into education that doesn't care. That thing about summers off is a bunch of BS. Anyone with that attitude doesn't get through student teaching. But if you want a career or if you need a steady job—which always happened to be the case with me—you learn to temper that caring. Or at least you learn to hide it.

So, for example, there was once an occasion where I had a student and their mother in my office. I began explaining to the mother that her

57

son had been a major disruption in most of his classes. He intentionally walked around with his fly open. He snapped girls' bra straps. He threw paper at teachers when their backs were turned. Really, it was unfortunate but rather typical middle school stuff. As I was explaining this to the mother she reached into her over-sized purse and pulled out a lead pipe about the length of my forearm. After she brought her arm back and made it apparent she intended to beat her son with a deadly weapon in front of his vice principal, I stuck my hand into the fray. She continued with the swing and shattered my left wrist.

I learned from that incident.

I'm not saying I wouldn't put my arm in between a student and a pipe if the occasion ever arose again. I'm only saying I would think twice about it. You understand what I'm saying? Caring is an instinct and teaching makes you pull it back a little, out of self-preservation.

Cynthia sat in a leather chair normally occupied by delinquent children.

"He was hanging out with Guy Callone," she said. "I shoulda stopped that shit. I knew from way back in the day that Guy Callone was bad news and when I seen my kid riding around in a car with him I shoulda pulled him outta there and beat his ass. Right on the street I should have beat his ass. What's a 13-year-old doing hanging with a grown-ass man?"

I wondered the same thing. All the answers I came up with were terrible, so I said nothing. She wiped her face and a new streak of eye liner went sideways to her temple. I'm assuming I gave her an accusatory glare because she followed her statement with a defensive shrug. "I had so much going on," she said.

Guy Callone. Yeah, I knew the name. I never had him as a student. He was a few years older than Cynthia, which meant he left the school before I had graduated college. Whether he ever graduated high school or not, I don't know. I heard plenty of other things about him from colleagues in the break room though.

He was a bit of a walking northern New Jersey stereotype, like a junior Tony Soprano. He was buddies with a lot of the guys that turned out to be cops later in life, but was way too much of a delinquent to become one himself. He set the bathroom on fire at the school. He walked around in tracksuits chewing on a toothpick even at twelve. He was on the wrestling team later when he was in high school and was the ringleader of a hazing scheme where kids got wrapped up naked in the wrestling mats and left in the locker room overnight—the mats duct taped around the kids.

What I had heard most recently was that he'd gotten involved with human trafficking.

"Do you know Guy Callone?" she said to me.

"I do not," I said. And that was the truth. I knew of him. What I didn't say was that I knew we had a mutual friend, me and Guy.

She went on to say she told her son she didn't think hanging out with Guy was such a good idea. She said this to him at their room at the shelter on the south side of town—a hell hole I knew well because in the past I had gone there to see for myself the conditions some of my students were living in. Henry had told her to go fuck herself, said she wouldn't know what a good idea was if it bit her in the ass. That was the last time she had seen him. She mentioned Henry had cash on him recently that she didn't give him. That made me swallow hard. What was Guy Callone paying Henry to do?

I asked her if she knew what he'd been doing with Guy. Had they been up to anything illegal that she knew of? She said no. Either she was clueless or she was pretending to be because she didn't want to face the awful situation her son had gotten himself into.

I asked if she knew any of his hangout areas. She told me the mall parking lot. In front of the liquor store. I told her I would tell the police to go by those places and ask for him. Her expectation, I knew, was that I would go look at those places myself.

She looked at me with pleading eyes. My eyes, I knew, looked back at her with fatigue. I had no interest in going down this rabbit hole, but no choice really. If I were a PI in an old film noir this is when I would have put my feet up on the desk and lit a cigarette. I was no Bogie, however. I wasn't even Jack Nicholson. I was a balding vice principal.

"You go to the police?" I asked.

"They don't care," she said, raising her voice. It reminded me of when she was a kid. She'd gotten in many a cat fight that I had broken up—pulled her away from another girl only to have her screaming at them over my shoulder - and that screech rang my ears like a bell. I still remember clearly the time Cynthia had a clump of another girl's weave still in her fist as I walked her down the hallway.

"He's a poor kid with a fucking junkie mother," she said. "He'll be just another body to them."

I had no idea she was a junkie. The way she said it, it was like she assumed it was a widely known fact.

I shouldn't have been surprised, to be honest. It was the path she'd been on probably since she'd been born. Being an educator, you see all sorts of kids. Some of them are born bright and they stay bright. Some of them are dumb as rocks but do okay for themselves. Some turn everything around and surprise you. Some of them, however, it'd be better for their own sakes if they'd never been born. Cynthia was probably one of those.

There was nothing else I could say to her. I wasn't going to promise anything. "I'll make some phone calls," I said. She left a sniffling mess.

That mutual friend I mentioned, the mutual friend between me and that scumbag, Guy Callone, he was known around town as Junior Twitchy. His older brother was nicknamed Twitchy because he had a nervous tick where his whole face would scrunch up. He would close his eyes real quick and wiggle his nose like a rabbit.

Because people aren't that creative when it comes to nicknames, especially nicknames for siblings, his little brother became known as Junior Twitchy. Never mind the fact that the younger guy didn't have a nervous tick like his older brother. He developed tick-like attributes - his hands would shake nonstop but that had nothing to do with plain old nervousness. It came, I assumed, from all the spray paint huffing he did.

Junior Twitchy, I knew, was some sort of look out or low-level shit-shoveler for Guy Callone. I'd seen them together often enough. I ran into Junior Twitchy on an almost daily basis. You see, even at my ripe old not so middle age, I had to get up hours before work and go over to the gym and hit the heavy bag. I would stop at a convenient store and get a few Gatorades and a protein bar. In the parking lot I would see Junior Twitchy sitting on a curb smoking a cigarette. We'd nod heads at each other and go about our separate business.

My plan was to get up a little earlier than usual and go pay a visit to Junior Twitchy, put him in the back of my sedan, hurt him a little, and see what he knew about Guy and Henry.

After I left the school it was already dark out. I went to the house I lived in by myself, fed my cat, jerked off in front of the internet, and then tried to go to sleep. I couldn't though, I was thinking too much. Thinking about my life. About Cynthia's life. About the things I believed in. About the things I had done.

Back when I had first met Cynthia I was a science teacher. I had gone to college for biology, was fascinated by evolution and especially the evolution of humans and our behaviors. I often talked to the kids about evolution even though it wasn't strictly part of the curriculum. The angry ones, like Cynthia, I would tell them that there was an evolutionary purpose to anger. I would say we get angry in response to fear. We see a threat and our bodies tell us to react in anger as a way to eradicate that threat. Therefore, I would say, if you want to deal with your anger, you have to deal with your fear.

Behind so many of our actions is an evolutionary purpose. Caring, the purpose for that is the well-being of our species. We care about one another because our collective survival depends upon it. Like anger though, caring can hurt you. Sometimes, the things that helped us evolve and survive as a species hurt us as individuals. Just like with anger, you have to learn how to cope with caring.

The incident that Cynthia remembered me for occurred before I learned that.

She was coming to school with bruises on her arms. One day she had a split lip. I often ran into her father at the off-track betting place I used to frequent in those days. He was a bulky lumberjack-looking sort of guy that always got into verbal arguments with the other gamblers. On more than one occasion those arguments came to blows.

After I asked Cynthia where the bruises were coming from and she told me they came from her being a rowdy sleeper who'd fall out of bed, I decided it was time to confront daddy-o. I was benching twice my weight at the time and had just earned a black belt in BJJ, so I wasn't too concerned about what he'd do to me.

I followed him to his car one night when he left the OTB. When he was getting in I put my hand on the back of his head and slammed it on the metal door frame. When he bounced back I used the force of his own bodyweight to bring him to the ground. I punched him once in the mouth and put him in an arm bar.

"I don't want to hear a fucking word from you," I said. "You understand?"

He nodded.

"No more hands on your daughter, okay?"

He nodded again and I let go. I stood up and he rolled over, got to his knees. Then I kicked him a few times in the ribs. He laid prone on the asphalt and cried. "That's in case you forget."

He started murmuring something in between the cries and the vomiting. "I didn't," he said.

"Sure you didn't," I said. Then I walked away.

The next day, Cynthia came to school with a black eye. I brought her out in the hallway. "Your father?" I said.

"My father was in the hospital last night," she said. "He told me somebody tried to rob him and beat him up. I fell out of bed."

"You fell out of bed and got a black eye?"

She looked at the ground and said nothing.

After school that day, I followed her on foot. I waited a minute after seeing her go through the front doors and then put on my coat and followed. There was a strip mall a few blocks from the school. She stood in the parking lot. A rusty pick-up truck that had wheels the size of my car and was covered in mud pulled up to her. She climbed in. Through the window I saw an obese man lean over and kiss her. It looked like he put his tongue in her mouth.

The next day after school I drove to the strip mall. There was Cynthia, waiting for her boyfriend. When the monster truck pulled up, I got out of my vehicle and went over to pay a visit. When I knocked on the driver's side window the dirtbag brought the glass down. Before he said a word, I opened the door, grabbed him by his shirt, and pulled him to the ground. I punched him in the ear and dragged him a few feet by his shirt towards the sidewalk. I hit him in the nose, bloodied it but didn't break it, and then rested his head on the curb, picked up my foot and held it a few inches away.

"If I see you around one of my students again," I said, "you're going to be eating through a straw until they're actually legal to date."

Judging by the wet spot on his jeans, I assumed he understood.

I made Cynthia get out of the vehicle and walk back to the school. I paid for her to get a cab home.

Now, what bothered me about that incident wasn't that I made that fat slob boyfriend piss his pants, but that I had put her father in the hospital. A piece of shit he was, but I didn't think he deserved the broken ribs. So, from then on I had promised myself to think a little more before I acted on a student's behalf, to be more even-keeled. In short, again, I learned I had to check my caring.

Thinking through those old memories, I wasn't able to sleep. The alarm clock said 3am. It was as a good a time as any to pay a visit to Junior Twitchy.

Driving over to the convenient store in the dark, I hit something with my car. There was a thud and then I saw a shape go off into the long grass and bushes at the side of the road. I pulled over, took out a flashlight and went over. After a minute of searching, I found a deer. Poor thing looked like a baby. It's back two legs were shattered. It was crying. It was suffering.

My gun was in my glove box. I could have walked back, gotten the piece, and put the poor thing out of its misery. I just couldn't. I was a coward. Instead, I got in my car and drove off, hating myself the whole way.

When I pulled up to the convenient store and saw Junior Twitchy, I was shaking a bit like he was.

"Hey. How you doing Mr. V?" he said to me when I approached. He couldn't see the wrench I had in my jacket pocket. "You still working over at the middle school?"

"Yeah, I'm still at the middle school. They made me Vice Principal, in fact."

"Aw, that's great. Climbing up the ladder."

Making him uncomfortable on purpose, I stood there and looked him right in the eyes for a good minute without saying anything. Then I motioned to my car with a tilt of my head. "I want to talk to you."

Once inside the car with both of us sitting and the doors closed, I whacked his knee with the wrench. The blow didn't shatter any bones, but it had hurt him enough for him to know I wasn't fucking around. He sang like a caged bird. "There's a rundown motel a few miles south off the Parkway. Place is essentially run by Guy Callone and his crew," Junior Twitchy said. "Place is like a brothel," he added when I threatened to go at the other knee, "only some of the workers are there consensually and some of them aren't." Henry, Junior theorized, could be holed up there on a non-consensual basis.

I pushed Junior Twitchy out of the car and drove off. Angry at the possibility of Henry being kept in some rat trap motel and forced to do God only knew what, I had to get to the gym and hit the bag. After an hour of hard rights and softer lefts on account of the old pipe injury, I headed home to shower before work. Driving, I saw Cynthia standing on the side of the highway. I cringed, but I wasn't surprised. She had on what looked like a fake fur coat and fishnet stockings. Her skirt was so

66

high that if it were light out and I were closer I would have been able to see pubic hair—as long as her johns didn't prefer her shaven, that is.

At school that day, there was a little scuffle between two eighth graders. One was calling the other's mother a lesbian, so the offended kid threw a lunch tray at him sideways and hit him in the eye. I had to have the kid that threw the tray sit in my office for a while to calm down while the school nurse looked at the other. The boy that sat in my office, his name was Craig. Seemed like a good kid. "Don't let people get the best of you," I told him.

The rest of the day I thought about Henry. I didn't know the kid at all, hadn't once interacted with him, but I figured that after all he was going through, he probably wasn't going to come out a good kid. And I thought about Cynthia. Should I have picked her up off the side of the road? I didn't because I didn't want to confirm what it was she was doing there. And also, I thought about the deer.

I drove down to the motel Junior Twitchy told me about around one in the morning. I had a picture of Henry that Cynthia had given to me, though I wasn't sure how recent it was.

Except for a light on in the lobby, the motel looked like it was closed. There wasn't even a sign with a name for the place anywhere in sight. If not for Junior, I would have driven by never knowing it existed.

I parked my car right in front of the glass doors that led to the lobby. There was an Indian woman at the front desk. She looked at the photo of Henry that I brought with me and said she'd never seen him. I took out my gun and tapped it on the counter, told her to look again, closer.

"Room 155," she said.

"You might want to get out of here," I replied.

Down towards the end of the hall, I saw a big goomba in a suit walk out of a room and leave the building. He was the protection, I imagined, and he decided to take a break from protecting. It could very well have been Guy Callone himself, but I couldn't tell having only seen the back of him. All I know is he came out of room 155.

Keeping my weapon in front of me with two hands, I kicked in the door. "Get on the fucking ground," I said, before I could even make out what was what in the room.

Over by the window was a chair with somebody tied to it. Someone was in the bathroom, clamoring for something. "Get the fuck out here," I said.

And they did, but when they did they came out firing. It was some old guy that looked like he could have been a vice principal himself, balding and out of shape. He was shirtless and in a pair of sweatpants. I got hit twice and went to the ground. From the ground, I looked up and pulled the trigger, twice. The old guy fell and the room instantly smelled like fresh excrement.

I went over and untied Henry. He was wearing a pair of white underwear that I didn't think people wore any more. He started to cry.

Looking at me, he said, "Can you just shoot me?"

I thought about that baby deer and how it suffered for the rest of its short life. I thought about how Henry's life would be if I took him out of that shit hole. He'd never recover.

"I can't do that kid. I can't," I said.

He looked like he was only partially there, only part human. What would he become? Would he become an addict like his mother? Or, would he become a criminal like Guy Callone? Or something worse?

Stepping away from him, trying not to look at him too much because it hurt to do so, I said, "I'm going to go. I'm not going to shoot you, but I will leave the other gun here. You do what you need to do."

And from the gunshot I heard when I was leaving the motel lobby, I assumed he knew exactly what he needed to do.

I took two in the upper part of my chest, near my shoulders. One in each lung. I should have died. No one could believe I drove myself to the hospital. I spent damn near a month there and damn near another month in rehab learning how to breathe without coughing up what was left of my lungs.

As old as I felt, I wasn't old enough to collect my pension. So, I went back to work.

On my first day back at the middle school, Craig, the kid who had thrown the lunch tray on my last day before I was shot, got into another fight. He was in my office, sitting there in tears. I said to him, "I don't care what your excuse is. You either get your act together, or you don't. I don't care."

The thing was, I wasn't sure if that was me pretending or if that was me being real.

I'm still not sure.

***

JUVIE

ANDREW BOURELLE

On summer days, me and Spider would walk along the Rio Grande and throw rocks at the water. The river wasn't much more than muddy brown puddles in those days with the drought and all. We'd tromp around, finding our way across, dig up old junk that was buried in the mud. None of it was treasure, but we'd act like it was. Bottles. Tires. Weird stuff too: a blender, a ceramic cow head, a snow globe. We'd haul the stuff around for a little while and then toss it.

We used to harass some meth skanks that hung out down at the river park by Central. These girls couldn't have been twenty yet, but they had yellow teeth and were skeleton thin. When they were all there, we'd call them names, the grossest things we could think of, and they'd yell back, telling us we had small dicks and saying we liked to jerk each other in the woods. But when this one girl was alone, she'd call us over and talk to us, flirting with us a little bit. Telling us what handsome young men we were. She wore these super short cutoff jeans and had bruises on her legs like some kind of purple oil stain was seeping through her skin from inside her body. She always wore tank top shirts with no bra. She had greasy hair that hung down around her shoulders, kind of like in old videos of Ozzy Osbourne from his Black Sabbath days. Spider and me always walked away from our conversations with her and joked about how gross she was, but I was secretly in love with her.

On the day it all happened, we saw her alone at the park, sitting on the bench with her knees pulled up to her chest.

"Hey," I said.

She looked up and offered us the faintest of smiles. She was paler than usual, and her smile made her look even worse, like someone on her sickbed trying to cheer up the people visiting instead of the other way around.

"What's wrong, Tina?" I asked.

That was her name: Tina. I thought it sounded kind of like a porn star name.

"Nothing. You got a cigarette?"

Spider had three and although those were supposed to last us all day, he doled them out and the three of us sat smoking.

"You guys got any money I can borrow?" she said.

We shook our heads. We never had any money. By the afternoon, when we got hungry, we usually went to a gas station or one of the supermarkets and stole something to eat.

"Look, guys, I need some money. I'm willing to do stuff for it."

"Like what kind of stuff?" Spider asked, taking a drag off his cigarette and acting all matter of fact.

"I don't know. Blow jobs." She shrugged and smiled coyly. "I'll let you stick it in if you've got enough."

"It's too bad we don't have any money," Spider said, as if this was just some normal conversation. "Maybe next time."

I wanted to ask how much, but I was too afraid.

When Spider and I took off, he started joking about what a disgusting whore she was. But I was trying to figure out if she'd was serious or just playing with us.

*

When we got bored, we'd go and throw rocks at the runners and bikers on the paved path that ran along the river. Sometimes we'd

72

miss so bad they wouldn't even know. Other times, we'd zing 'em good. We'd argue about who was the better thrower. Spider said I couldn't hit water from a boat, but I threw a couple good ones now and then, enough to make me believe I was at least in the same league with him. But the truth was Spider had a hell of an arm and fantastic aim. He could hit what he was aiming at—stationary objects, like trees or road signs—but he could also *anticipate* where something moving was going to be.

On that day, the first rock he threw was an all-time beauty, sailing out in front of this couple who were zooming toward us on their bikes. I thought for sure he'd led them too much, but the rock—flat and sharp—seemed to sort of float and wait and then speed up again just when the time was right. He hit the woman right in the side of the neck. She veered off into the gravel, and her wheels slid out from under her. She had one of those bikes where her shoes clicked right into the pedals, and she didn't pull out in time. She bit it hard, sliding in a spray of gravel and crying out in genuine pain. Her boyfriend or whoever it was who was riding with her gripped his brakes and slid to a stop. We took off, laughing. The guy yelled at us to come back. Idiot. Like we would do that.

We hid under the bridge on Alameda. When we heard sirens and realized they were coming to the parking lot at the trailhead, we climbed up onto the roadway and walked down the street like nothing was wrong.

We went to Enrique's Gas and Sundries (whatever a sundry is) to get out of sight. We'd knocked off a dozen gas stations already that summer (we had to pick a different one each time, in case they had security cameras), but we'd never been here. My job was to distract the clerk—Spider would fill his pockets. We'd never hit this one before because it was kind of a run-down piece of shit. The parking lot was always empty, and the convenience store inside seemed pretty small. It was one of those gas stations where, when you pass it, you might not be sure if it was still open or if it had been closed for a year. Come to find out, they made most of their money selling heroin right from behind the counter, but Spider and I didn't know that at the time.

The bell rang as we walked in the door. The clerk, a chunky Navajo chick, gave us a glance, saw we were kids, and looked back down at a magazine she was reading.

The place was a dump. Tile floors that looked like they were last mopped in the 1980s. Panels missing from the ceiling, exposing pink insulation and rusty pipes. A sign hanging on the restroom door said, *WHAT PART OF OUT OF ORDER DON'T YOU UNDERSTAND?*

Spider and I looked at each other and nodded, knowing what the other was thinking: no way this place had security cameras.

We were wrong about that, of course.

"You hear all them sirens?" I asked the clerk.

"I hear 'em," she said, bored.

She was flipping through an issue of *Rolling Stone* or some magazine like that. She seemed so unobservant that I probably didn't need to distract her anyway. But I liked my role in our little heists so I kept going.

"I saw what happened," I told her. "A girl wrecked on her bike on the Bosque."

"Yeah?"

She didn't look up. I glanced toward Spider and saw he was shoving magazines up under his shirt: *Playboy*, *Penthouse*. I didn't see if he grabbed a *Hustler*, but that was my favorite.

The clerk flipped the page.

"A coyote ran out in front of her," I said.

I love making up stories. The trick is to use some real information but to decorate it with crazy details. People believe the most out-there stories if you just tell it right.

"She must have hit the front brakes instead of the rear because she went flying over the handlebar," I went on. "Almost hit the coyote."

The clerk looked up, made eye contact with me, and glanced over toward Spider. She went back to her magazine, and I got the impression she didn't actually see either of us. I found out later she was as high as a hot air balloon.

Spider was filling his pockets with candy.

"Cracked her head on the pavement," I said. "I guess that's why they tell you to wear a helmet. I've never seen so much blood."

"That's too bad," she said absently.

If all the other shit hadn't happened, Spider and me might have celebrated afterward that this was our biggest score yet. Out of the corner of my eye, I saw him grab two bottles of beer. First a Coors Light and then he actually closed the cooler door, opened another, and grabbed a Sam Adams. Then he walked toward the door like everything was normal. What balls. He was holding the beers on the opposite side of his body from the clerk, but still you could see them. In fact, it was pretty fucking obvious that his pockets were bulging with magazines and candy. Either he was pregnant or he had a big bag of Doritos under his shirt.

She never looked up. He just walked out the door.

I wonder what the police thought when they saw the security camera. It really didn't matter at that point, but I bet they got a laugh out of that part.

What happened next is kind of a blur because I didn't see the guy come in. And I don't remember the bell dinging 'cause the door opened. The guy must have walked in before the door shut behind Spider.

Our plan always culminated in me saying something to the clerk—something real off the wall—and then bolting for the door. Then, when I hooked up with Spider out back by the dumpster, always out back by the dumpster, I would tell him what I said and we would laugh our assess off.

I probably wouldn't have said nothing if I'd known someone else had walked into the store.

"Hey," I said to the clerk, loud, to get her attention. "Can I get your phone number?"

She looked up, completely unfazed, as if I'd asked her if she had change for a twenty. Then her eyes rose up to something behind me.

A hand came down on my shoulder, clamping me hard. I immediately thought cop, must be a cop. "I you're a little young for her." A man's voice, deep and gravelly. There was a bit of a nasally sound, like he had a cold.

The clerk leaned back and gasped.

I craned my neck to see what had caused such a reaction. The guy's face was deformed, brown and flattened, as if someone had tried to mash all his features down with a ball-peen hammer. Or maybe he'd been burned in a fire and all that was left was this brown, smooth scar tissue. Or maybe …

He had panty hose over his face.

He pulled out a gun (a .38, I found out later) and held it up for the clerk to see. Then he cocked it and stuck it to the back of my head.

"I want the money in the safe," he said to the clerk. "You know the combination, so don't act like you don't."

She stared at him, not making any move toward any safe.

"Freddy?" she said.

There was a pause, as if we all needed a couple of seconds to figure out the meaning and weight of what she'd just said.

I remember thinking this guy must be an idiot for not wearing a better disguise. I guess he was probably thinking about how he was going to have to kill her now. And even though she was stoned to the meat bone, she had probably figured that much out too.

"Grace," he said, kind of growling, like he was talking through clenched teeth, "open the safe or I'm gonna splatter this kid's brains all over the counter."

She moved then, squatting down, practically out of sight. All I could see was the top of her head.

I never really felt scared. I didn't think I was gonna die. I guess that was my youthfulness, this feeling of invincibility. To be honest, when I realized he wasn't a cop and that he was gonna rob the store, I felt relieved and strangely exhilarated. I remember thinking that I was going

77

to have a cool story to tell Spider. Right now, he was out back, leaning against the dumpster and chewing on some Starbursts, with no idea what was going on with me.

He was going to be so bummed that he missed this.

Grace was piling stacks of bills onto the counter. I couldn't believe how much there was. Didn't these people know what banks were for?

"That's it," she said, rising.

"Put it in a bag."

She pulled a plastic bag out, just like she would for a customer, and started shoving the money into it. When she was done, she pushed it toward us. She didn't lift it and hand it to him, she just pushed it away like a meal she didn't want to eat, and then she wiped her hands on her apron, as if they'd touched something sticky.

"I won't tell them it was you," she said.

She didn't raise her head.

"Grace," he said, real calm. "Look at me."

I felt him pull the barrel away from my skull. Then the gun was next to my head. I could see the barrel out of the corner of my eye, pointed at her.

"I never liked you," he said.

The gun made the loudest noise I'd ever heard. I put my hands to my head and bent over. When people said their ears were ringing, I thought that was just some kind of expression. But it's true. That's all I could hear—a constant ringing noise, like the tone on a TV when there's an emergency.

There was a hole in Grace's shirt, up by her collar bone, and a dark wetness was

78

spreading from the hole. She leaned against the cigarette rack behind her, knocking all the packs onto the floor. The guy shot again, and this time I hardly heard the sound, just this muffled crack. A puncture opened in the fleshy part of her arm, like someone had gouged her with a screwdriver. A trickle of blood came out, then a whole flood. He aimed again, but she fell down. Just dropped.

Dead weight.

The guy grabbed me by the hair and made me look at him. He was trying to say something to me, but I could hardly hear it. It was kind of like when you put your head underwater in the bathtub and your parents are yelling for you but can't make out what they're saying. I'm pretty sure he was telling me not to say his name to the cops. I don't think he planned to kill me. I nodded like I understood.

I don't know how I heard it, but I did. Somehow through the ceaseless ringing came the distinct ding of the bell at the doorway.

Freddy spun around, bringing the gun up, ready to blast whoever just walked in. He stopped. His body sort of relaxed. It was just a thirteen-year-old kid with baggy shorts, a retro Slayer tee shirt, and stolen beer bottle in his hand.

Spider.

The guy laughed. He said, "You scared me kid."

My hearing must have been coming back.

The guy reached toward the money, and that's when Spider made his move. He cocked his arm back and, just as the guy was turning back toward the door, he flung the beer. The bottle spun through the air like a throwing knife, and the bottom hit the dude square in the face.

Direct hit.

The bottle didn't explode like I thought it would. The guy started to fall. The gun went off. Spider jerked his head back like he'd been pegged with a rock. The bottle hit the ground and that's when it broke—an explosion echoing the gunshot.

I fell on top of the guy, grabbing his arm and trying to pull the gun out of his hand. His nose was bleeding, tentacles of red slithering over his face inside the panty hose. He was dazed and trying to sit up. I only had a couple seconds before he was going to get his wits together and overpower me.

I put my mouth over his wrist and bit as hard as I could.

"Ouch, you little—"

But the gun was free. I couldn't believe how heavy it was. I jammed the barrel right up against his chest. He froze. We stared at each other.

"Wait," he said.

It took a lot of finger strength—more than I expected—and I watched the hammer rise up out of the gun and then, when my finger passed the point of no return, the hammer snapped back and the gun kicked against my hand.

I don't remember the sound of that shot at all, but I did hear a whoosh of air—sort of a reverse gasp—come rushing out of the guy's mouth. His breath smelled like wintergreen chew.

I shot him again.

And again.

I pulled the gun away from him and rose up. I pointed it at his head and cocked the hammer back with my thumb, just like someone in the movies about to deliver the coup de grace. This time the trigger was easy to squeeze. But the gun only clicked empty. It didn't matter. The guy wasn't moving. Blood bubbled up out of his chest like a spring.

Spider was still lying on the floor. The hole in his forehead looked like a little smudge of mud. Blood trickled out one of his ears.

If someone had walked in right then, I would have been declared a hero. Hell, they probably would have put me on the *Today Show* or *Good Morning America*. Maybe that Megyn Kelly would interview me. But there weren't any cars in the parking lot, not a single one filling up at the islands, nobody pulling in, no pedestrians walking by. I was all alone with three dead bodies.

I took the money and ran.

I'd like to say it was all worth it, that when I went to the park, Tina was there and we ran off and got a hotel. We fucked and drank and partied until the money ran out. And then the cops caught up to me trying to slip into Mexico. That would have been a better story. But the park was empty.

No sign of Tina.

I almost dumped the money in the river—leave it for some other kids to find one day—but I figured that would have been a waste. I didn't have Spider to help me steal now, so I was going to need money to buy snacks and magazines. I just went home, hid the money in my dresser with my *Playboy*s and *Hustler*s, and took a shower to get the blood off. When my parents came home from work, I was playing *Call of Duty* and acting like nothing special had happened that day. I almost felt like nothing special had happened—I didn't get to lost my cherry to Tina anyway.

I acted stupid when the cops showed up at eleven that night. If I had just taken the money and split, I think they would have let me go. They might have just said, "What the hell was this kid thinking?" and laughed it off. Or maybe they would have said I'd been through a traumatic experience and signed me up for therapy. I'd be spending my summer days walking along the Rio Grande, skipping stones, maybe getting a blowjob from some skanky meth chick, not in here, looking out the window at the desert hills and spending my days jabbering with y'all.

But after they seen the videotape, what else could they do?

I watched it in court, the camera giving a sort of high-angle view from behind the counter. The image is black and white, but it shows me, clearly me, grab the money, take a step, and stop. You can tell, even in the video, that I hear something. I look over the counter and see that the clerk—the chubby sexy Navajo chick—is trying to sit up. I glance out the door then I take the time to pick through Freddy the dead guy's pockets to find more bullets. I figure out how to open the gun. I load. I lean over the counter. You can see me cock the hammer back. It's harder than it looks. Then there's a flash of white in the gray video image. The girl's head jerks, rolls to the side, and then stills.

I wiped the gun and put it back in Freddy's hand and took his money.

I told the judge I didn't know the boy in the video, and he accused me of perjuring myself. That's a legal term for lying, my lawyer said. I wasn't trying to lie though. I was just speaking abstract-like. You know: figuratively. I guess the truth was even a little more complicated than that. I didn't know the boy who walked into that convenience store, the boy I'd been before. He was gone for good, just a picture on the screen, harder to recognize than if he'd been wearing panty hose over his face.

But the person who walked out? The one with the bag full of money and the taste of blood on his lips?

Yep, that's me.

And they ain't gonna keep me locked up forever.

AN ANTHOLOGY OF NOIR

SWITCHBLADE

ISSUE

GOTTA SHOW 'EM YOU'RE REAL

ROBERT RAGAN

Homeless and starving, out in the cold. The plan was to throw a brick through the grocery store's window, go inside and get some food. If I had gotten caught, at least I would have had food and a place to stay.

But instead, I ran into one of my homeboys. Crazy Jack. Little spoiled rich boy, blaring rap with a confederate flag hanging from his truck. Hair slicked back, his eyes told me he was gone. Born with a silver spoon in his mouth, he could have excelled at something legitimate. But no, he chose to sell dope.

Once I even heard that he ratted on his own friends. Jack is a piece of shit, but he's not a snitch.

As we passed a blunt, I told him he didn't know a thing about the struggle.

"You can run to mommy and daddy when you need the re-up money."

"They cut me off. Now I have to switch up my whole game," said Jack.

Reaching, he opened the glove box and removed a chrome 9 mm pistol.

"Oh, you think you're bad now that you got you a burner," I said. "How much did that cost your parents?"

All business, no jokes—he brought up this Mexican drug dealer we knew and said, "Let's go stick him up."

Desperation covered his face as he said, "I need all that powder and weed."

Sitting back, I asked, "What's in it for me?"

Close to nodding, he said. "Help me and I'll take care of you."

As soon as we pulled into the trailer park, I got this bad feeling. Riding through we seen people out on their porch.

As we parked in Jose's driveway, Jack said, "Get out, let's do this."

We walked inside his house and talked with him for a few minutes. All I did was stand there. Jose, with long oily hair, spoke in broken English. "Man you call me! You don't just show up at my place." Looking both of us up and down, he asked, "Anyway, whatchu need?"

A middle-aged Spanish woman walked out of the bedroom holding a toddler. Out of nowhere, Jack snatches the small boy from his mother's arms. She rushed towards him but backed away as he pulled out the pistol.

I thought Jack went too far sticking the barrel to this little boy's temple. Regardless of how I felt, it worked like a charm. Jose handed over everything. A major loss but he had to with his child's life in danger.

Everything went smooth, we were in and out in no time. When we left, Jack was in a hurry and broke the speed limit as we passed a cop. I watched him pull out behind us as he turned on his blue lights.

Looking in his rearview mirror, Jack said, "I'm fucked," and pulled over. We sat there calmly as he handed the officer his driver's license and registration; knowing he smelled the dank ass bud we had been smoking.

Standing beside the road, we watched this cop search Jack's car. It didn't take long for him to find the duffel bag. Next, he felt under the seat and found the pistol.

Earlier, I said Jack was no snitch. Now, I don't know. Not after he refused to take the blame leaving me to get locked up with him.

The DA scared me, threatening to hand out the maximum sentence if I tried to take the case to trial. I gladly pled guilty and came out with a 24-month sentence.

*

On the yard at Neuse Correctional, I tried to stay quiet and mind my own business. A loner in a prison where everyone clicked up. I had maybe one friend in the entire camp. The first six months went by fast with no problems. But sure enough, trouble was looming.

In the dorm's dayroom, an older, grey-headed man and I sat playing chess. Old mother fucker was the man on that board. The shit had me pissed off. I was close and almost had him, then loud mouth Maurice, who slept on the top bunk above me, came to the table. Nearly drooling, he said, "Yo son, someone from another dorm was in here going through your shit."

Thinking of my sodas and cigarettes, I hurried to my locker, thinking damn...I should have invested in a lock. Sure enough, they got me. Standing over my shoulder, with his braids twisted too tight, this fake Crip Maurice said, "I'll point him out to you when we go outside."

I waited, then the time came and as we walked to the chow hall for the last meal of the day, Maurice grabbed me and pointed at a group of inmates talking. He said, "It was the nigga right there, the one with the tight fade."

Seeing his height and the size of his biceps, I almost said fuck it, let him have that shit. But if I had done that, then everyone would have thought they could get me.

At first, I was like I'll just check him. You know, confront the thief and call him out on his bullshit. That was a sure way to get rocked in the jaw. So instead, I'd be the one to get it poppin'.

It took two days to catch this smooth cat on the yard by himself. When it happened, I was walking towards him near the basketball court. He expected me to pass by, instead I moved in and hit him with everything I had.

Some of his boys witnessed this. I could hear them over at the weight pile.

As I looked over my shoulder, the thief hit me hard in the temple. Stunned I'm disoriented, and my vision was blurred, yet I realized that I was surrounded.

The first punch I took shook my brain inside my skull. I don't know who hit me next but my vision went completely black. All I can remember was stumbling backwards and struggling to stay on my feet. Somehow, I did.

Barely regaining my sight, I still stood with my fists clenched.

Guards came quickly and cuffed my hands behind my back. Wouldn't you know, each thug went with me to solitary confinement except for the one who stole my shit. He just stood there next to this towering inmate watching as they took me away.

Thrown in a small isolation cell, it took no time to pass out after taking those punches. Waking up the next afternoon it hit me, this small ass cell would be home for the next 30 days.

A voice, from the cell next to mine, came through the wall. A black man said, "Boy, you've got balls made of steel."

Amused, I asked, "Why do you say that?"

Answering, he said, "Word is you just stole off on the biggest Blood on the yard. Plus, you took a shot from Big Face."

A voice, coming from further down the hall, said, "Yeah, and we're gonna fuck him up when we all get out of here."

The guy in the cell next to mine said, "You gotta give the man his props, he's the only one ever hit by Big Face who wasn't knocked out cold."

The voice from further down asked, "Hey white boy, ain't you in C dorm?"

I answered, "Yes." This person tells me there are two Bloods in my dorm.

He said I have to fight them both as soon as I get out of solitary. Plus, Big Face will literally try to knock my head off my shoulders the next time he hits me.

The voice coming from the cell next to mine said, "Boy, you better check off and ask 'em to place you in protective custody."

For 30 days, I was threatened and told I was getting mangled once this time was up. They asked me, "Yo, white boy, are you Crip or with the Folk Nation or something?"

"Hell no!" I said, "I'm not in any street gang. I'm just a white guy who caught a tough break."

They seemed to respect me once I told them how my co-defendant and I went down with a gun and dope charge after just getting away with robbing a Mexican drug dealer.

*

The day they let me out of solitary confinement, my feet were shaking in my boots; *for real, no bullshitting.*

90

Walking to the dorm, I was thinking, hey, maybe they'll let this whole thing slide. They'd already taught me that I don't ever want to get hit that hard again.

Yeah right, that wasn't enough and the two Bloods in C dorm wasted no time coming to check me. One, a short stocky inmate with a bald head. He had paw prints tattooed across his chest. His partner had a five-point crown on his arm, as well as paw prints.

They told me, "It's on after lights out tonight."

I had put my filthy white hands on their OG and I had to pay for it. My grave was already dug. Saying Fuck it, I told 'em they better bring it.

"Y'all fakes ain't even from California. What kind of Blood comes from NC?"

The taller one, with the afro, was ready to stick me with a jab right there but thought better of it once a guard had entered the dorm.

All-day long I dreaded lights out. Sitting on my bunk, loud mouth Maurice said, "You're fucking crazy son."

Checking him, I asked, "If you're a Crip, how come they never fuck with you?"

Before Maurice could answer, a look of terror filled his eyes. Glancing, I seen the towering black inmate who was standing next to the guy I hit that day. The two Bloods greeted him by saying, "Soo Woo."

This fucking giant, who they both called Big Face, was oiled up with muscles on top of muscles, walked right into our dorm and headed straight for me. Stopping just short, he told me to strap up then bent down to tie his boots.

Remembering the punch that made me blackout on my feet. I'm terrified of taking another one from Big Face. Yet, I stood my ground and didn't run.

I tried to think of anything to get me out of this situation. I said, "I never wanted any problem with you guys." Pointing at Maurice, I said, "This fake Crip right here told me your boy stole shit out of my locker."

Speaking up, a couple of inmates informed me that Maurice had been the one who stole my belongings. Listening in, the two Bloods rushed Maurice and ripped off his brown uniform shirt.

The taller one held him in a full nelson while the other examined his tattoos.

Reporting to Big Face, the shorter one said, "Yeah, he at least wants to be a Crab."

Face, with dreads covering his eyes, said, "Looks like you got set up white boy."

Pointing to Maurice, he told me to settle the score. "If you lose white boy," he said, "I'm gonna knock you the fuck out."

No waiting for lights out, I ran up on Maurice pushing him against the locker. My left hand slammed the back of his head against the steel. My right fist bashed his nose and mouth numerous times before the guards came and took me back to solitary confinement.

As they pulled me away, I saw Big Face and the two Bloods from the dorm standing over Maurice laughing as his blood gushed all over the floor.

This time, when I got out of solitary, I suddenly had this reputation.

To hear people say it, "Your boy done went to prison and fought the Bloods and Crips."

Aryan Brotherhood members told me they needed a badass like me down with them.

I told them I wasn't a racist and that I was only taking up for myself.

They didn't like being turned down. Luckily, my reputation had them reluctant to try me. Always a loner, I didn't want to click up with a gang. No, I just wanted to do my time and get the fuck out.

***

©2020 Robert Ragan

93

He nudges the pile of chips towards the cashier, a middle aged Asian woman with sharp black eyes.

"How would you like it, sir? In hundreds?" she asks, her unblinking eyes focused on him.

"Yes, please."

He leans on the rail watching her thin fingers skillfully counting the notes and bundling them carefully while punching numbers on a tablet screen.

"Your money, sir." She pushes the thick wad of cash through the slit for him to collect and flashes a brief, cold smile.

"Thank you," he says, stashing the thick wad into his leather purse. A minute later, clutching the purse under his armpit, he steps outside, through the revolving doors of the BLUE CASINO leaving behind the scented, dry air in the building, where too many people sneeze, cough and smoke. Outside his lungs fill up with the cool night air and he relaxes, a feeling of calmness invading his body, the stress from the night of gambling gradually dissolving.

It's 3.47 am and he's exhausted. Outside, in the open and quiet, is a bliss, because he doesn't smoke, he doesn't drink much and he doesn't socialize. He avoids any bad habits as he is a man with a plan, and he is close to accomplishing it. His heavy purse is the of evidence, another successful night of gambling at the roulette table. Only roulette. Nothing else. He specialized in chips pinching and he managed to master it to perfection.

But first of all—doing his time-consuming research on casinos with relaxed security. The main battle is the one before the real one. With this in mind, he made a list of all the gambling joints where he could practice his craft, the sleight-of-hand tricks. Well, con artists like him palm chips and either add them to a winning bet or remove them from a losing play. He is skilled enough to fool even the most vigilant croupier.

Also he often used past posting—the trick of waiting for the ball to land in one of the pockets, then covertly placing a late bet. This, often difficult to pull for the other cons technique, was a child play for him. Another favorite of his technique was pinching. This also required waiting for the ball to come to rest in a pocket, but instead of posting a late winning bet, the losing wager was removed from the table. And despite the various security systems by the casino owners that surveyed players, equipment, and employees to prevent most of the common types of roulette cheating, it didn't stop him. His delicate, fast fingers were built for that. He knew he was born for this. Like they say, there are two important dates in your life; the first when you were born and the second to find out why. He knew both answers.

He used to work with partners, some roulette dealers and other swindlers. However, someone else knowing your secrets is a bad idea. So he decided to play it solo making it rule number one: two can keep a secret if one of them is dead. When he mastered the ropes, he ditched all his partners even stooping so low to double-cross some of them. A bit brutal but he had to make it all on his own.

In this game you work alone, make money on your own and retire quickly and he was very close to the seven-figures he needed for that. He had already chosen, the place of his retirement—a small but nice, quiet property in Anguilla, in the outskirts of The Valley. Three more hits and he, at the age of 36, would be done with "working" in life. His fingers softly slide over the purse under his armpit.

Well, it could've been better tonight if it wasn't for that young bitch, quite drunk who threw tantrums while playing aggressively. This almost threw him off his game plan. Most of the women in those joints were arrogant and rude, most likely influenced by MeToo and all that feminist crap in the media. Despite that he wasn't a misogynist. He didn't have anything against women, of any kind regardless of, age, race, or profession. Even strippers and exotic dancers were okay, they were part of the gambling flora and fauna and sometimes, but very rarely, he used their services. After all he wasn't a monk.

However, he was focused on his retirement plan, it was hard work and distractions would only derail him. So, he had to stay focused on the ball and less distractions like women.

He steps off the curb and starts walking towards his car, an unremarkable black Nissan. He doesn't want to stand out, to be noticeable by anything. No, he needs to be the 'average Joe' in order to make it quietly and to survive in this jungle run by the noisy, arrogant men. He knows that nothing about him stands out and he keeps it this way. He is always clean-shaven, his black hair is neatly combed, and he usually wears black pants, grey dress shirts, and a sand-colored sports coat. Yes, his strategy is different and so far it has been serving him well. He knows that even reaching his goal in life he still will lay low and be the unremarkable man. Nowadays the quiet, focused guy is the winner. Not standing tall, rolling with the punches.

Well, the downside to this is being alert all the time, feeling lonely, without a friend or a woman next to him. A price to be paid.

He reaches his car parked in the far end of the parking lot, a corner lit by a blinking, dim sodium light.

He unlocks his car and slides behind the wheel, the moon a huge orange glowing through the windshield. This reminds him of Anguilla and he sinks in the seat, dreaming of a distant exotic beach where he will retire and will stare at the moon's reflection in the ocean's waters for the rest of his life. Smiling to himself, he stashes the purse into the specially designed pouch inside the seat with the tiny, well-hidden zip lock. He knows that the hideout is not perfect at all, but it will buy him some time in case of emergency. And the cash won't stay there for long anyway. In the morning he'll add it to one of his two growing offshore secret accounts.

A bump jolts the Nissan, forcing his head to snap back. Damn, did someone hit his car?

He moves his head from side to side to shake off the sudden strain in his neck. He turns with an effort, the pain in his neck pulsating. Through the back windshield filters the shape of a reversing white Toyota. A woman frantically gets out of the offending vehicle, her hair a halo in the street light.

He swears and carefully slides out of the Nissan. Outside, he locks his car and eyeballs the woman stepping towards him.

"I'm sorry..." she cries and throws her hands in the air, "It's too dark couldn't see properly, damn parking lot…"

Ignoring her tantrums, he examines the damage. A shallow dent on the fender, the plate numbers half scraped, and a broken tail light. He brushes the peeling paint and straightens up. "I need the details of your insurance, Ma'am?" he says, moving his head from side to side, trying to ease the pain.

"I'm really sorry for the trouble, it was really dark, I was in a hurry, you know, I'm running late..." the woman whines, her eyes on hi

"Your insurance company, Ma'am," he says, irritation intruding into his voice.

"Well, I don't have a current one, just expired. Today. I was going to renew it but..."

"You're leaving me no choice but to call the cops," he grinds his teeth and fishes out his cell phone from his jacket pocket.

"Wait! Do you really have to call the cops? About a fender-bender?" She steps closer and points at his car.

"This fender-bender will cost at least nine hundred dollars. The lights are gone, the plate is damaged. It's unsafe to drive..."

"Look," she interrupts him, lowering her voice, "Is there any way that we can resolve this without involving anyone else? Just the two of us, you know?"

He slowly raises his eyes from his cell phone.

"Anything that I can do for you?" she pauses, "Anything at all?" she says very slowly, stretching the vowels, as she steps closer so he could take a proper look at her. The street light illuminates her curly dark chestnut hair shadowing a wide face, with eyes fringed with long dark lashes and wide plump lips. A short dark purple dress with a deep cleavage, red fishnets on a pair of strong well-shaped legs and white stiletto shoes. She has the look of an exotic dancer, and her unblinking eyes say she knows it.

For a brief moment he forgets about his car trouble, while staring into those dark eyes.

"C'mon, darling, we can resolve this between ourselves, right?" she whispers, her lips first stretching then their corners turning up in a faint smile.

He keeps staring, caught in a slight surprise about such an offer.

She lifts a finger and delicately traces the outline of his jaw. "What's your name, darling?" Her voice breathy now.

"Bart," he says and stares back at her amused.

"I'm Donna. I like you, Bart."

She steps closer and her hot, strawberry scented breath floats in the air. He inhales, his eyes riveted at the smooth curve of her dark lips.

"Let's go," she whispers and reaches for his hand.

She starts leading him, stepping in front of him, her stilettos softly tic-toeing on the path. He stares at her from behind - hair, delicately bouncing on her shoulders, short dress, nice butt, legs stepping one in front of the other, on a straight line, confident and strong. He wouldn't mind following her, the short walk to the Casino's motel, like the joy that guilty pleasure brings. Why not. He deserves a small celebration after a night of hard work.

At the reception he books a room and pays the desk clerk, a fat old woman with dull, bulging eyes. He pays with American Express and with key card in hand follows Donna to their room number twenty-seven. In front of the door without hurrying, she gently pulls out the swipe card from his hand and unlocks the room. In the darkness she slowly draws him close, feeling his heart hammering. Moments later she detaches from him, turns the lights on and leaves her tiny purse on the small desk next to the window. When she steps back to him, he is motionless, waiting for her to snap him out of the spell.

"Relax, honey," she whispers, and her breath burns his face. While still holding his hand she slowly turns her back to him and presses herself into him and starts grinding her butt onto his groin. Her thick hair brushes his face.

The tingling in his loins is all needles. "God!" he whispers.

Her hand cupping his trembling hand starts guiding it, first up, around her breasts, then it slowly moves down her chest, her flat firm tummy, down the edge of her dress, then under, pushing inside between her thighs, touching the bottom of her hipsters. "Enjoy, darling," she whispers, "I'm yours now."

He reaches for her dress, clumsily unzipping the back, suddenly pulling feverishly. She doesn't resist, she is all but soft and obedient, a doll in his hands.

"I'm yours," she keeps whispering, and he bewitched, is an animal now –hugging, squeezing, biting her.

"Don't rush, enjoy the ride with a stranger, I'm not your wife," comes her breathy voice again.

He frantically slides her dress to the ground, awkwardly stomping on it. She, half naked, turns and faces him. While he bites the firm smooth skin around her neck, she undoes his belt, his trousers slipping to the ground. He nervously unbuttons his shirt, strips off his t-shirt, and his underwear. He is hectic, grabbing for something craved for a long time.

*

4:35 am glows on the radio alarm on the small desk next to her purse. She looks at Bart, snoring gently, mouth open, smiling in his sleep. His love making didn't last long—a couple of minutes, like most men. They enter you and a minute later they explode, releasing their load.

Too quick.

She learned to take it as a compliment. Well, she knows their button. That's all.

Anyway, he'll sleep for at least the next five hours. She knows this from experience. He just needed one pill - enough for a man with his slight frame. Size really matters here, not his dick size of course. She smiles. Once she needed to waste three pills on a huge guy to get him dazed.

The procedure, very simple, a pill covertly dissolved in the mini-drink bottles from the fridge for guests. Cheers to us, darling, lets drink it in one gulp, like the Russians do. No issues there, she's done it dozens of times.

She gets out of the bed, barefoot and reaches for her purse. Inside she carries a very light, tiny cell-phone. A lifesaver.

A text from Timmy glows on the miniature screen. 'cant sleep mom. im playing clash of clans'. He knows that when she is working, she can't answer. As a good, seven-year old boy, he follows their strict agreement to text her every couple of hours, letting her know what he is doing. And he is allowed to do whatever he wants except leaving the house. Until she gets home.

She slips her cell phone back into her purse and checks Bart's jacket. Except for two credit cards and a cell phone there is nothing in his pockets. She doesn't trust credit cards. Only cash. Bart's wallet must be somewhere in his car.

She pats his pants. In the front pocket she finds a ring with two keys only and a medallion with Nissan's logo. Bart looks like a careful man- no other keys for an apartment or bank lockers. Just car keys. They will do. Once the job is done she will return them to his pocket.

In the night light, she catches a glimpse of herself in the mirror. Her hair is messy, one of her long eyelashes twisted, mascara smeared under her left eye. She feels sticky and she desperately needs a shower but this will come after the job is done. Then she will collect her stuff, the empty mini bottles and cleaning up everything, leaving nothing behind pointing at her.

She dresses without hurrying, brushes her hair with a hand, and at the door she checks on Bart sprawled on the bed. Sweet dreams! Men. Weak creatures. One fuck and they melt like an ice-cream in the sun.

Outside the corridor is quiet, only her steps muffled on the worn-out carpet. That time the casino patrons have gone to bed except for a few stubborn players dreaming of winning over the machines. A bunch of suckers chasing the wind.

She finds his car, her's a foot behind. Despite the damage the Nissan's trunk lock is still working. She checks inside, by habit, in case a bag full of cash lays there. The trunk is almost empty except for a box of tools, a set of golf clubs and a jack. A tidy man this Bart guy. She shuts the trunk and looks around. The empty parking lot relaxes her.

She unlocks the driver's door, slides inside and turns off the interior light. She doesn't need light to check for the hideouts. Her sharp eyes expertly examine the interior, her fingers swift in checking the seats, the sides, front and underneath. Her fingertips touch a zip not fully closed. She slides a finger inside and through the widening gap, she touches something. Her heart flutters. Sweet feeling. Her heart keeps hammering when she pulls out a heavy leather man's purse. The wad of cash inside is not a surprise to her. She turns on the interior light. All Benjamin's, between forty and forty five grand. Heavens! A sweet catch. Well, that's her specialty, shadowing gamblers, watching them cashing in at the counter, then bagging them. Like this one, Bart. She got him in the bag pretty fast.

She turns off the interior light and, intensely peering through the windshield, looks around for any people outside. With this load of cash she must be on alert now, avoiding any trouble.

Carefully stepping outside, she locks the car, drops the keys in the leather purse with the cash and clutching it tightly she starts walking towards the back door of the motel.

When she is close, the ajar door catches her attention. A strong arm snakes around her neck from behind and jolts her back. Startled she gasps and pushes forward, her heart like a punching hand on a wall. The arm tightens a

104

notch, a vice of death. A burning breath hisses, "What you got in there, sweetheart?" Another arm slides down her chest and snatches the purse from her hand.

"Heavy, eh?" The voice, although just a hot whisper, drops icicles down her spine. "Well," the hand weighs the purse. "A nice catch tonight?"

The thick arm is blocking her airflow, making her struggle to breathe. "Well, honey, let's get inside and have a small chat. And don't try nothing stupid."

The arm unclenches and spins her around. She, still gasping for air, faces a solid man. A complete stranger. Short haircut, clean shaven, square face. Black jacket, dark shirt and matching dark pants. Despite the darkness he wears yellow glasses, like Bono's from U2.

He nudges her towards the door, opens it and pushes her inside. "Room number?"

"Twenty-seven," she croaks, her throat tingling from pain. They move down the dimly lit corridor. Damn cheap motels, she knows there are no cameras, no patrons, there won't be anyone coming to her rescue tonight. She steals a look around but as if the man reads her mind says without hurrying "Don't try nothing fancy!" His finger like a steel rod pokes her in the ribs, making her shiver.

Their steps, muffled on the dingy carpet, reach the room. She swipes the card and opens the door. He pushes her inside and closes the door behind. He takes off his yellow glasses and slips them inside his breast pocket then unzips the purse, turns it upside down and drops the contents on the floor. "Car keys and a nice brick. Is that your retirement? Lifesavings? You count it?"

She doesn't answer.

He pockets the key ring, and thumbs through the wad, whistles slightly and stashes it into his jacket pocket. Gets up and looks at Bart spread out on the bed.

"What we got in here, Barty? You work with a partner?" He pushes her towards the corner and steps to the bed where Bart snores, mouth open, hands wide spread with not a care about the world. Unsuspecting what will hit him very soon.

The man reaches for Bart's jacket, checks inside. He finds the two credit cards and pockets them. He stares at Bart for a long moment before he slaps him. Bart moans softly and keeps snoring.

"What did you give him, sweetheart?" He slaps Bart harder across the face with the purse. His head sways to the other side, Bart moaning slightly. The man slaps him harder. "Wake up, fast fingers!" He stares at him. Bart opens one eye and tries to focus. "What's he taken? What did you give him? Red Birds?"

She says nothing, stepping from one leg to another, uneasy in the corner. The man smacks Bart hard with the back of his hand. "Hey, asshole!" Another smack and Bart straightens in bed.

"Where is the money, asshole? The loot from the Gold Pot?"

Bart's eyes focus and he seems to recognize the man in front of him. "Roper? Wait! What loot?" he makes a slight attempt to evade but the next thing is a strong punch in his solar plexus, making him gasp and folds in two. He gags and the bile dyed substance colors his lap. Pungent stench of spew drifts in

106

the room and mixes with the disinfectant from the bathroom.

"The big loot asshole? Don't make me repeat!" Roper bends over Bart and his thick fingers wrap around Bart's thin neck like a pair of pliers. A steel brace. Roper squeezes. "Where is the stash?" He keeps squeezing and Bart shaking, vomits again, chocking in his own puke. His fingers start tapping like a dying rabbit. Roper eases his clutch. "Where?"

"In the... Cayman Islands..." Bart chokes again, gasping between refluxes of vomit and convulsions.

"Where in the Caymans?" The clutch is back even tighter and Bart collapses. The man slaps him. "You'll die here, you asshole. Where?"

Roper releases his neck and Bart gasping, whispers, "The Fidelity bank ..." And he starts babbling the bank details.

"Slowly!" Roper commands and pulls out a cell-phone from his pocket. Without hurrying, with one finger he punches while Bart repeats the digits. Then Roper dials a phone number. "It's me," he says into the phone, "Check the account," and he dictates. "Call me back." He ends the call, pockets the cell-phone and looks at Bart, head slammed down in his hands, saliva and vomit drooling down his chin.

"If the numbers don't come right I'll snap your neck like a match, you know that? It's only money, eh," he says, his mouth twisting in a sarcastic smile. "Ain't worth dying for money..."

Bart nods very slowly, the drooling down his chin stretches like a rubber band, his eyes turning inside his head. When Roper asks for the pins of the two credit cards, Bart is quick with his answers.

107

"I'll tell you this for free, stealing from Mickey Cuomo's Casino was the dumbest thing you ever did, asshole. He wants to talk to you, just a small chat, you know."

Bart says nothing,

"To have a close look at your famous fingers, this thin finger together with the wrists and forearms and the arms." He pauses, "You know what I mean, you fucking dumb ass." Roper grabs Bart by one arm and drags him out of the bed, like a dirty rug, keeps dragging him across the floor into the bathroom.

While watching Roper slamming Bart into the bathtub, she steps backwards towards the desk, grabs her purse and hastily stashes it under her dress into her hipsters. Exhaling deeply and closing her eyes for a moment, she suppresses the instant adrenalin rush.

In the bathroom Roper fishes out a pair of plastic zip locks and ties Bart to the shower tap. He kicks Bart in the ribs and closes the bathroom door.

Back in the room he eyeballs her, turned towards the wall, her eyes closed, avoiding the ugliness of the scene.

"C'mon, honey we have work to do." Roper pushes her towards the door.

"Look, I have nothin' to..." she protests weakly and he slaps her across the face.

"You almost got away with tonight's dumb Bart's loot, eh, you whore?" He cracks a smile that doesn't suit him at all.

She stares at him, the well-dressed Roper, all muscles and no soul.

"If you was me wouldn't you try to do the same thing?" Suddenly she toughens, looking square into his eye, taking him for precisely what he is—the muscle of some rich asshole. She knows his type very well. Just two buttons for Roper. Punch and fuck.

    "Shut up, bitch!" He slaps her and she realizes he is from the one-button guys. Only punch. Fucking is not exactly his button, so she goes quiet. She won't try any erotic tricks on him. He is immune to that.

    "Whores and swindlers. Fucking losers," he mutters while dragging her out of the room. He hangs up a 'Do not disturb' sign and grabs for her. His fingers dig deep into the flesh of her arm in the sensitive area for inflicting maximum pain. She clenches her teeth suppressing a scream.

    When they reach the Nissan he unlocks the car and shoves her inside.

    "Where're we goin' ?" she asks huddling in the corner.

    "How about withdrawing some extra cash from Barty's cards? He won't need them no more. I bet you know how to do this, eh? Your face on the ATM camera not me? It's a pretty good idea. And then we will have a good chat how you know about Bart, and you gonna tell me all, 'cause I hate grifters. Mickey Cuomo will have a chat with you too later. So, embrace for a long night ahead, honey." He puts on the nice smile again and turns on the car keys. The engine growls and before he releases the brake he pauses. He slowly turns off the engine, pulls out the wad of cash, leaves it on the dashboard, and looks at her.

    "Where exactly did you find this little brick?"

    She doesn't answer clenching teeth embracing for the onslaught.

    He slaps her in the face. "Where, bitch? Don't make me ask again!"

A sudden thought springs into her mind. "In the trunk," she says, "Under the spare tyre. There is a secret compartment."

"Did you check the whole trunk?"

She swallows. "Didn't have the time to…"

"You always got to do the things by yourself. Can't trust anyone," he murmurs while getting out of the car.

She hears him opening the trunk and thrashing stuff. Out of the corner of her eye she catches his reflection in the rearview mirror pulling out the spare tyre.

Her heart jumps in her throat as she lunges for the ignition and with a roar, the engine starts. She pops it in reverse and jumps on the gas pedal.

The jolt of the car is brutal and the dashboard hits her in the shoulder like a boxer's punch, instantly followed by the muffled cry of Roper, sandwiched between the Nissan and her car.

She yanks the gear into drive and releases the gas then jams into reverse and slams again onto the man collapsing on the asphalt. She repeats the maneuver, and gasping for air, adrenalin blasting through her veins, she scrambles out of the Nissan. A few agonizing seconds before finding the courage to peep behind the car.

Slammed to the ground, Roper's a mess, something from a slaughterhouse, face smashed to a pulp, one eye fallen out of its socket. In the dim light something almost black streaming down from his nose and mouth.

Suppressing a wrench in her guts, swallowing hard she looks around. A deserted parking lot. In the far corner only three cars, maybe belonging to staff.

Her initial impulse nudges her to get into her Toyota and speed away, but she pauses, knowing that her first instinct is always wrong. Focus!

Her phone? Her car keys? Here, here! Hastily she fishes her purse out of her hipsters.

Seconds later she snatches the wad of cash from the Nissan and scrambles into her car.

There, in the darkness, breathing heavily she thinks hard. Roper's dead. Just a guy overrun on the parking lot early morning, maybe by a drunken driver and left to die. It could be an accident it could be a robbery or a fight. These things happen every day. The gambler's in the bathroom locked, alive. Even if she frees him he'll talk. The receptionist saw them, her fingerprints in the motel room and in the Nissan. Damn. There's no way out this time. The only thing she got is the head start and forty-five grand. If she plays her cards right it may take them awhile until they get to her.

She turns on the ignition.

***

©2020 George Garnet

The old pissin' wall? The side of a rundown, red-bricked building on 4th once housing a wholesale vendor of cheap, stuffed animals. Purple bears and yellow frogs given as prizes at carnivals and amusement parks. Years ago, Timo Vela and his buddies relieved themselves in the alley between it and an aluminum-siding warehouse. In those days, they ran meth for Mr. Losa to rich gringos in Beverly Hills and West Hollywood. Most of the guys he'd worked with back then caught bullets for trying stupid shit in federal neighborhoods. Now, Timo collected on bets gamblers made with Mr. Losa. During October, football, baseball, basketball, and hockey stepped on each other's toes. The risk junkies piled debt they couldn't honor. No time to find parking at a legitimate establishment, sneak in, and hope nobody noticed him using the toilet without making a purchase. The old pissin' wall would have to do. Timo had just scraped a white-haired mayate's forehead across the jagged surface of an unpainted picket fence in Koreatown and he had less than an hour to make a house call in Long Beach.

He pulled to the curb, forcing a homeless mother and her son to jump onto the sidewalk, and got out. Newspapers, fast food wrappers, cardboard boxes, and a potpourri of other garbage crunched beneath his feet. Collapsing pup tents lined crumbling storefronts. The air reeked of human waste and decay. He ducked into the alley and found a space between metal trash cans glued to the ground by petrified filth. As

113

he unzipped and sprayed a faded Taylor Swift concert bill posted on the wall, something rustled to his right.

"The fuck?" He kicked away a sheet of crusted bubble wrap, revealing a battered young woman. She reached up, tried to speak. Blood stained her swollen, potato-shaped face. He moved more garbage away from her. She'd been dropped in the alley naked. Pink welts, purple bruises, and crusted gashes decorated her body. Her long, blonde hair had matted to her shoulder. Despite the hell she'd endured, her wide, ocean-blue eyes glowed under the Los Angeles sun. When her throat found air, she produced only a croak.

Timo stepped to his left and finished pissing on the wall.

*

He ripped south on the 710 in his sputtering Kia. Any time traffic clustered, slowed, he whipped onto the shoulder and snuck past the confusion. He veered off the highway and zig-zagged the streets of Long Beach until he arrived at a beige, one-story apartment complex on Bird Avenue. Looked like it might have housed so-called respectable middle-class families in the 1950s. Timo didn't know about the economic status of the other residents, but the hippie he'd been sent to collect from, a hefty Cleveland-transplant called Cornbread, barely earned the nickels necessary to pay his football debts. Timo parked out front and climbed over the wooden gate leading to a tiny, square patch of concrete behind Cornbread's apartment. The stench of Cornbread's three undisciplined retrievers lingered outside his sliding glass door. Timo made eye contact with him. The hippie's panicked glare suggested he'd gotten a notion to run but hadn't done so in time. Timo rapped the glass with his knuckles. "Open up," he said. His voice, in these situations, reminded him of his father, a Desert Storm veteran who'd dropped dead from a brain parasite Timo's senior year of high school. His father had not approved of the direction America had gone after September-eleven.

"Country's soft," he'd said. "Nobody wants to take responsibility for their own actions. Bunch of fucking twelve-year-old girls calling themselves men."

He'd believed in corporal punishment and beat Timo any time he found dope in his room. "Don't you know this shit turns you queer?" He'd wave the baggie of grass, or pills, or powder, with one hand and used his other to sock Timo in his mouth. He often split his lip. A few times he'd blasted him hard enough to turn his nose into a faucet. Timo's mother would suggest he avoid making his father angry. Timo had threatened to go to child protective services, threatened to tell his teachers whose classes he barely attended. In response, his father slammed a thick PVC pipe into the side of his face. "Say some shit like that again. See what happens." He said Timo should fight his own fights. "You want to show me who's boss? Bring it. Otherwise, appreciate who puts food on the table and a roof over your head."

Timo had sworn he'd pay his father back. Someday. Then, in 2008, his father passed out while watching the Trojans throttle the Irish on television. Two weeks later, he checked into Kaiser-Permanente. Scans never paid for showed his brain had dissolved like a clump of cauliflower in a bowl of soda pop. After Timo's father died, his mother returned to Guadalajara, leaving Timo to battle Los Angeles on his own.

Cornbread opened the glass door. "Hey man..." The forced smile, the genial tone in his voice—indicators he didn't have the money. Three bony mutts fussed over a chew toy so mangled it no longer resembled anything identifiable. Torn and faded posters of Huey P. Newton and Mao Zedong hung halfway on the walls, rolling over where tape holding the corners lost grip. The moist fragrance of unkempt dog nearly suffocated Timo. Smelled worse than the Toy District. He held his nose and spoke:

"Browns lost."

"You're telling me." Cornbread ran his fleshy fingers through a glob of unwashed, gray hair framing his face and hanging past his shoulders. "They always find a way, don't they?" He scratched at a dried chocolate stain covering an image of Mickey Mouse with a Hitler moustache on his T-shirt.

"Not my concern." Timo retrieved a small, leather-bound notebook from his back pocket. He opened it to a marked page and pointed to the ledger. "You thought they'd cover. They didn't." He tapped the figure next to Cornbread's printed name. Fifty dollars.

Cornbread shifted his head left and right, like the arm on a metronome. "Yeah, man," he said. "Thing is, I got to take Bootsy in for a checkup. I think she's got worms."

"Who the fuck is Bootsy?" But he already knew. Cornbread pointed to one of the dogs. Told him the other two were George and

116

Mayfield. "Ten-percent per day," said Timo. "You know this."

"Aw, man. Give a brother a break."

"You're not a brother," said Timo. "You're a guilt-laden white boy from Cleveland. A pandering, condescending heir to Manifest Destiny. I'll be here tomorrow for the fifty-five you now owe us."

"If I don't have it today, what makes you think I'll…"

Timo wrapped Cornbread's greasy hair around his fist and shoved his head into the metal frame on the glass door. Blood bubbled and spilled from his nostrils, colored his mouth and chin tomato-red. "We go through this shit every time," said Timo. "Mr. Losa's had enough. Said I should crack your skull, you pull your usual weasel shit. I were you, I wouldn't worry about that stupid fucking dog. You got something in your wallet? Anything at all?"

Cornbread disappeared into his bathroom. He wept as he ran water over a towel and wiped off his face. Waiting for the dumbass to return, Timo watched a small television propped on a dinner tray in front of a couch with no cushions. A news broadcast cut to a couple of rural gringos. The announcer said they were from Regina, somewhere in Canada. A husband and wife, both sporting hair grayer than Cornbread's. They held up an air-brushed senior portrait of a porcelain blonde named Marilyn Lambert. Said she'd run away, wanted to be a movie star. Timo tried to convince himself the girl's wide, ocean-blue eyes were not the same he'd seen in the alley by the old pissin' wall. Last thing he needed. Some conscience trip. Didn't the girl's parents understand? Your daughter flees for Los Angeles,

117

kiss her goodbye. The best thing that could happen to her? A quick, painless death. An overdose at a party attended in effort to blow a producer for a walk-on role in the next J.J. Abrams abortion. Maybe she hooks up with one of the five million psychopaths in Southern California. He cuts her into pieces and distributes her across the 15, like rose petals down the aisle at a wedding ceremony.

Nope.

Not his problem.

Cornbread emerged from the bathroom holding the soaked towel over his face. He spoke through it, his voice muffled. "I got twenty I can give you today."

"Great," said Timo. "Tomorrow, I'll come back for the other thirty-five."

*

The rest of the day went pretty much the same. Losers trying to negotiate their way out of either paying or taking a beating. Usually both. Timo imagined himself no different than his father, distributing pain the way a priest offered the host at church on Sundays. Don't have Mr. Losa's money? Hold still. This is going to hurt. A *lot*. He'd grab a chair, a butter knife, a Barbie doll, transform it into an instrument of torture. A trick he learned from Bruce Lee's book on Jeet Kwon Do—*anything can be a weapon*. When he got home, his girl Corina told him to fix a couple of cans of ravioli. She'd been in her studio, working in a Garfield T-shirt and torn American flag panties with *Fuck Trump!* written in sparkly letters across her sculpted bubble-butt. She'd bathed in blue and yellow acrylics. Some art project involving painting lewd pictures into history

118

textbooks she planned on presenting at an exhibition produced and attended by so-called L.A. hipsters.

In the kitchen, Corina's tiny, transistor radio had been left on, tuned to a talk station. She enjoyed listening to conservative pundits bemoan what they called "the browning of America." Code, of course, for the diminishing population of gringos who didn't know how to come when they fucked. Timo reached over to turn the dial. Days he returned home with multiple shades of blood on his knuckles, he preferred 1260, the oldies station. The innocence of early rock and roll, hiding its hormonal engine in metaphors, allowed his mind to wander to a place where Los Angeles looked clean, like it did in black and white movies. A place where people like him, his angry father, his negligent mother, Mr. Losa, the degenerates he collected from every day, didn't exist. He held off, however, when the ultra-serious female DJ announced the Lambert family had offered a five-hundred-thousand-dollar reward for the return of their daughter.

Corina entered the kitchen. She'd scrubbed the paint off her hands and switched out Garfield for Hello Kitty. "They talking about that crudo bitch from Canada?"

Timo tried not to wince. His girlfriend must have noticed him looking away. She said, "What, you give a shit?" She laughed and helped him open the second can of ravioli and dump it into a pot on the stove. "These bitches come here all the time, end up floating in the ocean, cut to pieces in the park, whatever. Something happens to us, they don't talk about it on the news. Why the fuck would I care when something happens to them?"

"You're better than that," said Timo.

119

Her eyes walked the ceiling one time before she said, "Make my dinner."

"They're offering a lot of money. Half a million."

"For what? That bitch is probably bleeding out on a table at some Satanic Hollywood party. You think you give them a corpse, they're going to pay you shit?"

"Someone they love is missing."

She shoved him out of her way. "You seem to think my dinner's going to make itself." She moved the pot back and forth over the flame on the stove. "Worrying about some fucking puta. Oh my God..."

"I think I know where she is."

Corina stopped working the pot. "You shitting me? You're kidding me, so help me, I'll cut your fucking balls off and shove them up your nose."

"She's by the old pissin' wall. I'm pretty sure."

Her face scrunched as she considered him, as though the veracity of his claim could be read somewhere on the legs of his jeans, or the clenched fist of an illustrated Darth Vader on his T-shirt. She shook her head and said, "Do not fuck with me, Timo."

*

They exited the 110 and crawled the streets at the posted speed limit. They wanted no attention from the police or the scattered zombies crazy enough to wander downtown L.A. at night. They coasted into the Toy District and Timo slowed near the old pissin' wall and parked. Most of the pup tents on the sidewalk were still, their occupants snoring like machines. A drunk staggered toward them, threatened to crash into Corina. Timo pulled her out of the way. The drunk, his face layered with grime, tripped and smacked his head against metal bars protecting a store with plastic army soldiers displayed in the window.

They turned the corner into the alley between the defunct stuffed animal vendor and the aluminum siding warehouse. An October wind rippled newspapers and hamburger wrappers spread across the concrete like a mismatched carpet. Rodents chirped warnings to their enemies. Timo put his hand in front of Corina, as though protecting her would somehow make the rodents disappear. She said, "The hell were you doing here in the first place?" He explained the pissin' wall, how it served as an emergency bathroom. "Disgusting," she said.

He started to rationalize his behavior, expressing his frustration with both the traffic in Los Angeles and the lack of public restrooms. He stopped, however, as they stumbled upon the young woman.

A pulsating moon dropped pale, blinking light on her lifeless body. How long had she been dead? Impossible to tell. Her skin had turned gray. Her wide, ocean-blue eyes, however, still commanded attention. Corina slapped her hand over her face. The stench from the woman's corpse seeped into Timo's nostrils and forced him to do the same.

"Oh my God." Corina stepped backwards.

Timo had experienced the fragrance of death before; the horrid odor stuck to the senses like a parasite. He leaned in and lifted his foot to nudge the girl, to make sure she would not move. As his sneaker hovered over her shoulder, a rat the size of a terrier poked its head from under her thigh

121

and hissed. Blood caked its snout. It had buried its face into the dead woman's flesh and clearly resented the interruption.

Corina screamed and ran out of the alley. Timo followed her, unable to hurl sound from his dried throat. They booked to his tiny car, got in, and slammed the doors, as though the rat had grown a hundred times its size and pursued them. He looked in the rearview. Nothing but steam rising off the pavement and curling around tents and trash cans. Corina's chest heaved as she spoke. "Never mind. Someone else can have the money."

"We can tell them where the body is," said Timo.

"And become prime suspects?" she said. "Are you stupid?"

*

October blended into November. Business rolled as usual. Corina presented her installation at a warehouse near Little Tokyo. The women wore librarian glasses and severe expressions suggesting they'd never taken a relaxing shit in their lives. The men had grown wild, lumberjack beards in effort, Timo suspected, to demonstrate they had *not* been collectively drained of their testosterone. They wore T-shirts adorned with pictures of Marx and Che. They clutched plastic cups filled with alcoholic punch and discussed the performance art as though they'd witnessed the Second Coming.

The news had stopped reporting on the grief of the Lambert family. No one collected the reward. No one offered a clue as to the fate of their daughter. Timo kept his mouth shut. Corina convinced him the people in charge of the world would blame him for the gringa's demise. "They'll say you killed her and lock you up." Timo had done nothing but break the law his entire life. How rich would it be to get busted for something he had nothing to do with?

The collision of sports seasons reached a stressful peak during the World Series. The Dodgers got their asses handed to them by Houston. Timo clocked eighteen-hour days bashing skulls for Mr. Losa as the degenerates of L.A. decided the Dodgers couldn't possibly blow their first shot at glory in thirty years. The more they protested, the harder Timo beat them. He nearly put Cornbread in the morgue when the hippie suggested Timo get psychological counseling for what he called "anger issues."

"You gutless fuck," Timo said as he broke the tank lid of Cornbread's toilet over his skull. "This is work, brother. Nothing more."

Eventually, he found himself downtown, in a traffic jam, needing to unload the gallon of coffee he'd consumed over the morning. He inched onto 4th Street and parked in a red zone. With the blinkers on, hopefully warding off tow trucks, he ducked into the alley with the old pissin' wall. He had not been there since the night the rat chased Corina and him from the dead woman's body. As expected, the corpse had been moved. Or maybe devoured by rodents. Oh well. Every motherfucker for themselves. Like that guy Darwin had said: *Survival of the fittest.*

He unzipped his pants and looked for a fresh spot on the old pissin' wall. The faded Taylor Swift concert bills had been covered by Have You Seen Me? posters. Marilyn Lambert's wide, ocean-blue eyes beckoned from each, identical picture. He aimed at her face and let loose. Something rustled in the newspapers surrounding a cluster of trash cans to his right. Could have been a rat. Could have been a bum. Timo finished dousing the Have You Seen Me? poster and zipped up. He returned to his car without looking back to see what had been moving in the alley. He tuned the radio in his Kia to a conservative talk station and laughed as ancient gringos lamented the fall of the Roman Empire.

***

©2020 Alec Cizak

The old man waits for his grandson to shit. He paces around a kitchen no bigger than a prison cell while the twenty-one-year-old strains in the bathroom down the hall. For an hour and a half, moans and groans have been echoing throughout the entire house, and the old man is relieved when the kettle starts whistling for him on the stovetop. He lifts it off a bed of blue flame to pour a cup of tea. The tea comes in a small packet claiming "constipation relief," and the old man hopes to hell it works as he marches toward the bathroom. Fed up, he knocks and enters.

"I don't smell shit," he says.

"Wish you could, bro. I haven't shit in about two weeks."

Looking like he just stepped off the set of *The Walking Dead*, Zack Fiasco sits and shifts his weight on the uncomfortable crapper. He scratches the blue-black needle marks on his wiry arms as cold sweat leaks through the cheap fabric of his Metallica t-shirt. Heroin withdrawal has got him fucked. Big time. If he'd only said "no" to the job, if he'd thought about the violent crew involved, he wouldn't be pinching a loaf while his grandpa tries to rush him out the door.

The old man hands him the cup of tea. Zack takes a sip.

"Ew," he spits. "The fuck is that crap?!"

"That, young man, is gonna make you feel ten pounds lighter. Drink up and you'll be shitting in no time, leaving too."

"Tastes as bitter as you are."

"Bitter? I'm not bitter. I just want you off the pot and outta my house. You think I wanna spend my evening with a punk like you?"

126

The old man didn't expect a visit from his grandson. Hasn't expected anyone to visit in over fifteen years. His bitch of a third wife had been put to bed with a shovel, and his grown children, sick and tired of his drunken behavior, never come around the neighborhood anymore. The only people who still set foot on his property are Jehovah's Witnesses, and the old man likes to greet them with a pump of his 12-gauge shotgun.

Solitude is fine with him.

"You need more fiber in your diet," he says, digging around the medicine cabinet.

"Yeah, yeah. I'll make sure to eat a bran flake or something."

"Catch." The old man tosses Zack a bottle of *Turbo Lax*. "If you don't like the tea, then chug that gunk. Otherwise I'm goin' to Walgreens and gettin' you an enema."

Zack's eyes go wide. "What?! No. I'm not stretchin' my asshole with a plastic hose."

Locked up at Cotton Correctional, Zack had done a three-year stretch for selling crack near a children's playground. Smoking it too. Hard drugs had eaten all of his baby fat – revealing high cheekbones and smoldering eyes—and the shower hawks on Block 6 wanted to run a train on his ass but never got the chance.

"Nothing's goin' up my butt," he says. "Nothing, like, ever."

The old man coughs up a laugh. "Just wait 'til your cellmate gets out. You know what they say, right? 'Once you go black…you get AIDS.'"

"Ha-ha, fuck you." Zack isn't tickled, not in the slightest. "My cellie wasn't black, and I ain't gay. I did suck some dick, though. We all did. There was this one dude named Barnes and, man, the only thing that took me out of it was when my balls brushed his stubble."

Thinking back on how Barnes used to go down on him makes his cock twitch. For a second, Zack wonders if he's one hundred percent homo but snaps out of it.

"No enemas," he says.

"Then drink the tea," the old man says. "All of it."

"Fine, bro."

Bro. The old man didn't go to Vietnam just to have a degenerate fuckup call him "bro." What the hell planet did the little cretin call home? He stomps out of the bathroom and gets a can of *High Life* from the fridge. Pops the tab, downs it, then grabs another two. The old man doesn't want to think about Zack's current situation. Doesn't want to think about the shooters coming after the kid, or the fact he's getting dragged into the middle of this himself.

Snatching up his untouched dinner, he scrapes off the grime for his mutt, Sadie.

"Don't think I forgot about you now," he says, tousling her fur.

The old man moves to the front of the house and looks out the panel window. His overgrown lawn is a burial ground for car parts, scrap metal, and broken furniture. Christmas lights have been dangling from the roof since '75 and, somewhere, there's an overturned clothes-dryer with a swarm of rats inside the drum. He wipes a layer of dust off the window and catches his reflection in the streak. Deep, fine lines carve into the valleys of his hollowed out face. *This shit is worse than Nam*, he thinks, *so much worse*. The old man hates to admit it, but having Zack barge in to drop a deuce is the most action he's seen in a long time.

"I'm not hearin' any splashes," he calls out. "That tea should be workin' its magic."

"Oh, something's workin' alright," Zack says. "It's just not workin' fast enough. My stomach hurts like a motherfucker, bro. Fuck!"

Sphincter gaping, Zack hunches over and squeezes until the color leaves his cheeks. He needs to hear the *Plop! Plop! Plop!* of things dropping into the bowl.

"It's not happening! It's not happening!"

It needs to happen.

If he doesn't shit soon, he'll die.

*

When he'd gotten out of prison a few weeks earlier, first thing Zack did was shoot a gram of speedball and head northeast. He licked the blood from his puncture wound as he steered his van toward Flint where, four miles outside the city, there was a bait shop called *Cheap Hookers*. The shop didn't hide that it was just a bottom-shelf liquor store with some fishing poles and a cooler full of worms. It was a front for a couple of rednecks with a hand in racketeering, drug trafficking, dog fighting, and murder.

A bell above the door jingled as Zack walked in and headed to the register. Behind it sat a tomato-faced fatfuck reading *Buns & Ammo* magazine. Zack waited while the tomato finished a section on "Machinegun MILFs: High Caliber Cooch." Finally, he flipped the page and said, "What do you want?"

"I'm lookin' for a dude named Pickett. You him?"

"Could be. What do you want?"

129

"Here for a job, I guess."

"You guessed wrong. Ain't no Help Wanted sign out front. Even if there was, we wouldn't hire some loser off the street."

Turning his attention back to the stroke mag, Tomato drooled over a woman fingering her pussy while sucking a pistol. Zack exhaled. He wanted nothing more than to get the hell out of there and get high, but knew he should follow through on the plan: Back in the slammer, after a steamy night of oral sex, he'd been told about the men Barnes used to roll with, and a good word would be put in with them once he was sprung. He'd be set. Money under the table.

"I was told I could get work here," Zack said.

"Uh-huh. Who told?"

"Barnes told me."

Tomato looked up, real surprised. "Barnes?"

"Yeah, bro. Dude said I should come to Hookers once I got out the pen. Thought he meant I should, you know, go and bang some working girls, but he meant to come here. Said I should ask for Pickett."

Tomato questioned him some more then came around the counter to feel for weapons. There were none, but he found a balloon of off-white powder and pocketed it before bringing Zack down to the basement.

The basement had all the comforts of a doomsday bunker, complete with cracked cement walls, dangling lightbulbs, and a 1980s television set. Two rednecks named Cooter and Purvis were sucking glass pipes and laughing at *Ren & Stimpy*. Another redneck lurked in the shadows and gutted fish that were laid on top of a chest freezer. He wore an M1 army helmet, whitey tighties and unlaced combat boots. With long brown hair and a wooly beard, he looked like Jesus had been blown up in a meth lab.

Tomato called to him. "Pickett! Got us a job interview."

Using a Rambo-like hunting knife, Pickett made cuts into the fish, scooped out their innards, then tossed them into a bucket with a wet *Splat!* He looked over his shoulder and gave Zack a hard stare. "So what do you want a job for?"

"I need the money, bro."

"You need more than that," he said. "It's showin' on you, boy. You're scratchin' your arms and you can't stand still."

Grin on his pockmarked face, Pickett approached Zack with the nine-inch blade. He ran his thumb along its sharpened edge and, with little effort, drew a line of blood. It was a silent gesture that said not to fuck with him. Ever. He came in close and his breath smelled as bad as the fish.

"Let me take a wild guess," Pickett said, scrutinizing him. "You think you're gonna come work for me and skim a little off the top, right? Build up your own stash. Get a free fix when no one's lookin'."

Truth was, Zack planned to do exactly that but was now rethinking his scheme. His head was all over the place, and he needed another shot of speedball.

"Look," he managed. "One of your guys said you'd hook me up after what I did for him in the joint. He can vouch for me."

"You a cop?"

The whole room fell silent. Zack tried to look unconcerned while the men fixed him with practiced looks of contempt.

Pickett continued. "If you're a cop, you gotta say so. You can't come in here and entrap me on some bullshit. And if you *are* gonna do that – man to man, cop or no cop – I'm gonna take this knife and fillet your pee-hole, understand?"

Zack wasn't too sure about Pickett's legal advice, but didn't want another circumcision.

"Understood, bro. The answer's 'no.' Not a cop. Do I look like one?"

Pickett narrowed his eyes. "You got the job, boy. Fuck it up and I'll kill you. Work starts now."

*

He cruised down I-75 and inhaled the fumes that came out of his broken exhaust pipe. Carbon monoxide made his head spin like *The Exorcist*, and the dizziness made him feel good and gone. Zack cracked open a can of Monster to sweeten the buzz. It was his third energy drink of the morning, but he still couldn't wash the taste of condoms out of his mouth. He'd swallowed a hundred of them. Each condom was filled with ten grams of decent-cut crank, and the rednecks had him moving the stuff into Canada by way of human suitcase. The job: make the trip, unload the product, then come back in for five benjamins a week.

Crossing the border with a phony passport, he passed through Windsor, the armpit of Ontario, and found the drop spot outside an abandoned gas station. There was a hooker motel across from it, so he figured he'd hole up in a room until it was time for the deal.

The room was a shabby little pad that smelled like dried sperm and cigarettes. Curtains were drawn, lights flickered, and the bed was a grid of rusty springs. Zack had spent a lot of time in motel rooms overdosed and covered in vomit, but this time, he believed, things would be different. He lumbered into the bathroom clutching his stomach.

Guts churned, but he smiled through the discomfort knowing there was meth to be shat and money to be made. Placing his hands on his knees, he started to push with a slow and sustained pressure. Rocked back and forth, clamped and unclamped.

Nothing.

After all his effort, Zack couldn't shit a goddamn thing.

The last time he was plugged up that bad was during a heroin binge with his girlfriend, Shakima. Between the two of them, they had shot almost four grams a day and were bloated from opioid constipation. Zack doubled over, held himself. Shakima groaned as if someone were giving her the Heimlich. They couldn't bear the pain anymore so Shakima stepped over to Zack and spread her pimpled ass-cheeks for him. A thick, dank smell wafted out of her, and Zack had to hold back from gagging as he dug his fingers in for extraction. Hand over hand, he pulled a monstrous shit out of her like ship line. After what seemed like forever, the colectomy was over...and so was their relationship.

Why hadn't he thought of that before swallowing thirty G's worth of meth?

About two hours had passed and he still couldn't go. Fishing through his bunched down pants, Zack untied a small bag of dope he brought with him. He realized drugs were the cause of his entire ordeal, but he also realized he hadn't had a taste in a few hours.

Plunging a needle in slow and deep, he let the soothing wave of heroin flow through his veins. Zack sighed with great relief and…

…drifted…

…until…

…the drugs started to wear off. He came out of his stupor with a sharp pain in his tailbone. Zack knew he must've been sitting on the crapper for some time, so he got up and peeked his head into the bowl.

Still nothing. Damn.

Walking out of the bathroom, he looked at the digital clock on the nightstand. The readout was faded, but it looked like he'd nodded off for a couple of hours.

Hours. Plural.

He missed the fucking deal.

His pulse began to rise and palms began to sweat. Zack felt like he'd stepped into an endless nightmare until a sudden vibration startled him awake. He reached into his pocket, answered the burner phone.

"You double-crossin' sonofabitch," Pickett said on the other line. "You think you're smart, do ya?! You think you can pull a fast one on me?!"

Zack did some nervous sputtering before getting his words out.

"Hey, bro, it's not what you think. I can't get the stuff outta me."

"Cut the shit, boy. No one steals from me! No one!"

"Steal?! Bro, the stuff is still inside me. Let me deuce it out and we can make the deal."

Pickett scoffed. "You must think I'm dumb, huh? Well, let me tell you somethin', asshole: I got my people lookin' for you. I even got the *buyers* lookin' for you. Ain't nowhere to run to, ya thief! You're fuckin' dead!"

Zack heard Pickett fumbling around on the phone before hanging up. In the short amount of time it took for him to realize he was worm food, he heard heavy footsteps outside. The buyers. Holding his breath, Zack pressed his ear to one of the paper-thin walls and listened to the sound of the adjacent room being forced into.

There was no place to hide. The only options were for him to go through the front door and get shot, or bust out the window and fall two stories.

He could've used another blast of smack as his chest rose and fell in a terrified rush. Zack scrambled into the bathroom and turned on the showerhead to cover the sound of him snapping off the towel bar. He headed back into the bedroom where he pressed himself against a wall, held his breath, and hoped the buyers were stupid enough to follow the noise.

That's when a hard kick ripped the door off its hinges. Two thugs stampeded into Zack's room, guns drawn. One of them rushed into the bathroom with an Uzi and emptied its entire clip in seconds. The other thug charged into the bedroom with a .45. He was so amped up he didn't notice Zack hiding in plain sight, clenching twenty-four inches of heavy metal.

The thug turned his head as Zack brought the weapon around and cracked his windpipe like a piñata. Blood began to waterfall out of the thug's mouth in a gagging wheeze. He grabbed at his neck with both hands and, before he could drop, Zack swung again. The impact shattered the thug's jaw as he hit the carpet. Zack jumped over him and raced out the door before the goon in the bathroom could finish reloading.

Lungs burned as Zack leapt into his vehicle and keyed the engine. It took a couple of seconds to get the tin can to start, and when it sputtered to life, he looked out the windshield and saw the goon on the walkway above him. A spray of bullets ripped through the van's roof as he backed out, shifted into gear, and sped down the road. He wasn't sure where he was going but he was getting there fast. For a moment, Zack thought about ditching his ride and stealing a new one before he got back to the States. Maybe get high and grab a prostitute until the heat died down. The fire in his gut told him it was a bad idea, though, and he wanted nothing more than to get the meth out of his body and onto the streets.

He had thirty thousand dollars to start a whole new life. All he needed was a safe place to take a dump first.

*

Zack takes a deep breath and lets his head hang low. He doesn't know how long he's been on the old man's toilet but knows he has to do something about it soon. He can't just sit there. His body trembles, and the sharp pain cutting through his intestines is only a fraction of what the rednecks will make him feel.

"They're gonna kill me, bro. They're gonna fuckin' kill me."

136

"Wouldn't be a bad idea," the old man says, flashing him a grin. "When a man dies, he shits himself."

Unamused, Zack keeps his eyes fixed on the linoleum floor. "How do you know that?"

The old man takes the cup of tea from his grandson, pours it in the sink. He knows all about the stench of death and shit – not just from Nam, but from when he caught his wife in bed with two teenage boys. His mind flashbacks to the night he blasted them in half with a 12-gauge shotgun, and their naked asses defecated on the blood- and cum-stained sheets.

"Trust me," he says, nodding to himself. "Shit happens."

They both fall silent and return to their own thoughts when Sadie starts barking at the front window. The old man stumbles out of the bathroom to see what she's going on about. He notices a white Bronco with all-terrain tires rumbling in their direction. It's enormous. It's ugly. It's affixed with the Stars and Bars. No doubt it's the crackers coming to collect, and the old man takes a second to shake his head at the insanity of it all. Why can't everyone just leave him the fuck alone? He's pissed that his house will be the stage for a white trash drama, and he'll have to play a part if he wants it over and done with. The old man knows it won't be pretty. Then again, his life has never been pretty so what's the difference? He calls to Zack, who has nothing to offer, then rips his shotgun off the wall, crams a pocket full of shells, and treads into the mugginess outside.

The Bronco races down the secluded drag and cuts a hard left onto the driveway, kicking up a wave of dirt and rocks as it comes to a complete stop. Pickett climbs out of the driver's seat carrying an assault rifle. Behind him are Tomato, Cooter, and Purvis, and they're armed to the teeth with pistols and bandoliers.

The old man does his best impression of stone. He doesn't want to have to shoot the bastards, but can see from the porch their eyes are bloodshot and crazed. No telling what they'll do. Their lips curl into canine snarls as the old man glares back at them, feeling the indignation build. If they come any closer, he figures, he'll need to draw first.

"The hell do you want?" the old man grumbles.

Pickett stands with a tight grip on his weapon. "Looks like you already know what we're here for."

"Nah, I just show this pump to anyone who comes on my property. Don't go feelin' special now." He keeps his shotgun pointed down but makes sure they hear its thunderous rack, *Ch-chak!*

"All we came for is a good-for-nothin' thief," Pickett says. "He took somethin' that ain't his, and I suggest you turn him over."

"Can't do that if no one's here."

Pickett points at a van parked outside the garage. "The boy drives an '83 Vandura," he says. "That model ain't too popular these days, and finding one here, in this town, is a bit suspicious."

"Hate to break it to you, Jethro, but the van's mine."

"The bumper sticker tells me it ain't."

The old man darts his eyes and notices the decal: CAUTION! THIS VEHICLE MAKES

138

FREQUENT STOPS…AT YOUR MOM'S HOUSE.

Goddammit.

"I know you're his grandpa," Pickett shouts. "You got the same ugly mug but a lot more mileage. Where is he?!"

The old man fingers his trigger guard.

"Occupied," he growls.

Zack has no idea what's going on outside. It sounds to him like some coked-up wrestling promo. He mutters curses under his shallow breath and hates himself for not steering clear of the needle. All he can do now is sit and squeeze.

Pickett spits a wad of tobacco on the ground.

"Listen, old man. I want you and your mutt outta my way! I only aim to kill the boy, but I'll blow the dentures out the back of your head if you keep interferin'." He shoulders his rifle into the firing position. "I'll let you chew on that."

"Chew on this!"

The old man raises his shotgun and cuts loose. His aim is meant for Pickett, but the blast hits Cooter in the chest and explodes his lungs out in a gush of blood. The kickback knocks the old man off balance and he falls down the wooden porch steps, rolling out of the way before the rednecks return fire. Bullets obliterate the lawn and chew into the house behind him. Heat rockets overhead as he crawls through the junk in his yard like the trenches in Khe Sanh. The old man leans up against a stack of truck tires for cover, and the rubber gets torn to shreds by a hail of scorching rounds. Reloading, he snorts air up his nostrils to slow the cadence of his jackhammering heart. "I'm back in the jungle," he tells himself, as a bolt of energy surges through him and he jumps out, pumping and firing.

It's the best he's felt in a long time.

He squeezes the trigger and turns Purvis into hamburger meat.

Then a small flash goes off somewhere, and the old man feels a blistering sting, suddenly aware of the gore oozing out of his left shoulder.

Tomato clips him with a Browning 380.

The old man staggers forward but manages to lift the shotgun with his one good arm. He butts the stock against his hip and shoots Tomato in the face, ripping him apart like blood-soaked confetti. Chunky head meat and hair splatter everywhere, hitting Pickett in the eyes and blinding him for a second.

The old man has his opening.

He pumps his shotgun but nothing goes into the breech.

Pickett wipes his face then steadies his aim. He fires, but the old man drops to the ground and pulls a pistol from Purvis's cold, dead hand. His adrenaline is wearing off and an incredible, searing pain consumes him. Fighting through it, the old man blasts into Pickett.

Bang! Bang! Bang!

The acrid tang of gun smoke hangs thick in the air. Everything is ghost-quiet except for the distant wail of police sirens. There isn't much time left so the old man stands up and dusts himself off. He limps over to the porch where he sees a lump of mutilated flesh.

Sadie. The bastards shot his dog.

The old man has never felt much sympathy in life, but seeing Sadie riddled with bullets makes his goddamn heart break. He can't stand the way his chest starts to tighten and

140

how his mouth feels dry. Furious, he storms into the house and glowers at Zack in the bathroom. Zack looks back at him, expecting the old man to help him move the drugs since he took care of his peckerwood problem. The old man just shakes his head. Standing there, leaking fluid and on the verge of losing consciousness, he thinks about all the things that have gone sideways since the little punk showed up.

The old man lifts his pistol and shoots Zack in the chest.

A gaping red hole forms. Zack opens his mouth to say something, but there are no final words. No final thoughts. Not even a moment to see a montage of his pathetic life flashing before his eyes. He exhales one last breath and slumps over on the crapper like Elvis has left the building.

And then it happens.

Sphincter muscles relax and an avalanche of shit-covered condoms comes roaring out of Zack—cutting a wet fart that trumpets for a solid minute until the room teems with putrid vapor.

Using his foot, the old man pushes his dead grandson off the toilet. He looks into the bowl and sees what so many people have been killed for. It's all there in a splattered mound, sitting for the taking. The old man thinks about how senseless it all is, about how everything in the world—family, love, age, and aspirations—turns to shit.

There's nothing left for him to do except flush it down the drain.

***

©2020 Danny Sophabmisay

SWITCHBLADE

100 PROOF
MODERN NOIR

OUTLAW
SINCE 2017
TALES
WITHOUT LIMITS
POLITICALLY INCORRECT

SWITCHBLADE

QUICK & DIRTY
ANTHOLOGY
OF NOIR
SHARP & DEADLY
LOS ANGELES

THE WORLD'S ONLY NO-LIMIT
NOIR DIGEST MAGAZINE

ACCEPT NO SUBSTITUTES

QUICK
&
DIRTY

FLASH / FICTION
FLASH / FICTION
FLASH / FICTION
FLASH / FICTION
FLASH / FICTION
FLASH / FICTION
FLASH / FICTION
FLASH / FICTION

Pornatoan
David Rachels

When Amber didn't come down for breakfast that morning, I figured she'd overslept. Again. I waited till the bacon was done before I went upstairs to wake her up.

I was annoyed, of course. Amber was an adult, which meant I shouldn't have to get her up in the morning. It was bad enough that I had to make her breakfast.

So I knocked hard on her door and waited for her to moan in reply, but no moan came. I knocked harder but still got no reply. "Get up, Amber!" I shouted. Still, nothing.

Risking one of Amber's tirades about her "privacy," I opened her door, which wasn't locked for once.

"Get up!" I said again, but then I saw that Amber wasn't there. I screamed, but I didn't scream because Amber was gone. I screamed because Amber had made her bed, and I screamed because she had left a giant double-headed dildo on her pillow, spotlighted by her bedside lamp.

My screams brought Roger running upstairs.

"Oh my god!" he said as he burst into the room. "She made her bed!"

Then he saw the dildo.

My husband walked over to the bed and stared at the dildo.

"It's wet," he said. "See how it glistens in the light?" He peered more closely. "*Both* ends! *Both* ends are wet!"

I was still in shock. "She made her bed," I said, "so maybe she washed the dildo before she left."

145

"Or," Roger said, "maybe there's DNA on that dildo."

"Oh, god, Roger, why are you even thinking this way?"

"You don't think this is a crime scene, Helen?"

"You mean some kind of sex crime?"

"I mean kidnapping."

"You mean kidnapping by pornographers?"

"Why else would Amber make her bed if she wasn't being forced at gunpoint?"

"Pornographers with guns?"

"Given the evidence at hand, that seems the most likely possibility."

I took a deep breath. "We should never have moved to Miami," I said.

"But I wonder," Roger said, as much to himself as to me, "why would a pornographer leave a dildo behind? Pornographers *need* dildos."

"And why would a pornographer force Amber to make up her bed?"

"*Excellent* point, Helen. Perhaps Amber was kidnapped by a pornographer with a sense of irony?"

"But if Amber *were* kidnapped by a pornographer, why would the pornographer want us to know that he's a pornographer? Why leave that disgusting clue?"

"Another excellent point, Helen! Maybe it's misdirection. Maybe the kidnapper is the *opposite* of a pornographer? What's the opposite of a pornographer? A poet, perhaps?"

"But what if the kidnapper *knew* we would think that a pornographer would never leave behind a clue that so obviously implicates a pornographer, so the pornographer decided to misdirect us by *admitting* to be a pornographer?"

"Pornographers *can* be crafty," Roger admitted. "That would also explain why he forced Amber to make up her bed—*misdirection by irony.*"

Roger kept staring at the dildo until I said, "I can't bear to look at that thing anymore. I'm going to get something to pick it up with and throw it away."

Roger grabbed my arm. "What? Why would you destroy the evidence?"

"Because it's disgusting."

"But the DNA, remember? We'd better call the police."

I hesitated. "But in the movies, kidnappers always say *not* to call the police."

"*Those* kidnappers want to negotiate for money. *These* kidnappers want to keep Amber and . . ." His voice trailed away. We both stared at the dildo.

I called the police. The officer who came addressed his questions to Roger.

"She's been gone how long?"

"She left sometime last night."

"And this is her sex toy?"

The cop photographed the dildo.

"Her mother and I have never seen it before."

"And there was no note of any kind other than the sex toy?"

"I believe there's *DNA* on the sex toy," Roger said. "When we found it, it was glistening."

"I'll bet it was," the officer said. He took a deep breath and said, "Folks, I don't disagree that your daughter is gone, but there doesn't seem to be any evidence here that a crime has taken place."

147

"Excuse me?" Roger said. "The dildo?"

"What about the dildo?"

"It didn't get there on its own!"

The officer stared at my husband, then looked at me.

"I think what my husband is trying to say is that our daughter would never have brought something like that into our home. It means that someone else was here."

Roger added, "We think it may have been a pornographer."

The officer looked back and forth at us. "And your daughter is an adult?"

"Yes."

"And there aren't any signs of foul play? Broken window, scream in the night, anything like that?"

I asked, "That sex toy isn't foul?"

"So the sex toy is all you've got?"

"And the bed," Roger said. "The bed is made up. She wouldn't have made up her bed unless somebody forced her to do it."

The officer closed his notebook. "I'm sorry, folks," he said, and he left without saying another word.

I started to cry.

"No, no, no," Roger said, "we've got this." He hugged me tight. "I'm putting you in charge of the dildo. Take it to a private lab, and find out if the DNA belongs to Amber. I'll take care of the rest."

I didn't want to know anything about the dildo, so I threw it away and lied to Roger about it. For his part, Roger now spends every night on his computer looking for Amber at every porno site he can find. Some nights he never goes to bed. He's spending thousands

148

of dollars a month on membership fees, and when I tell him we should be using that money to hire a private investigator instead, his answer is always the same.

"No, no, no," he says. "I've got this."

***

©2020 David Rachels

Hero
Elliot F. Sweeney

Dale emerged from behind the hawthorn, clutching his bag, shaking. His ears still pinged from the shotgun blasts. Cuts and nicks peppered his arms. With the harsh summer light beating down on his nape, he took in the aftermath.

A man lay outside the newsagents shop. He was facedown, his right-hand still clutching the sawn-off. Homemade tattoos marred his knuckles and arms. Blood was oozing from beneath his still chest. Dale knew what corpses looked like. He was seeing one now.

A few feet left lay a woman. She was on her back. Her eyes were open, staring at the blistering sun.

Dale's boots crunched on the broken glass as he came to her. 'Miss! Can you hear me?'

Her right leg twitched. She wasn't dead.

Pure instinct, he dropped his bag and crouched by her head. She blinked. Focused.

"You're gonna be OK." She was about his age, brown hair, brown eyes to match. He looked at the red puddle in her gut. "Can you talk?"

"Feels sore." She reached for the wound.

"Don't," He took her hand. 'Ambulance is coming. They'll fix you."

"You were fighting that man with the gun. I saw you."

He nodded.

"Is he dead?"

Another nod.

"What… what happened?" As she spoke, blood began trickling from her mouth.

Dale glanced around, piecing together the last few minutes. After the shooting and screaming and people fleeing in all directions, this roadside seemed eerily still.

"An armed robbery." He gestured to the newsagents. Glass dangled like teeth from the window. "The owner wouldn't handover his money. That robber lying dead grabbed an old lady, said he'd shoot her. I stepped in. We fought for the gun. He started firing. It was chaos. He kept shooting. bang, bang, and took the last slug in his chest."

She blinked. A milky caul was forming over her eyes.

Keep her talking, Dale thought. 'You remember much?"

"I'd just head out and heard yelling from the newsagents shop. Through the window, I saw you fighting. Heard the explosions. Then it felt like I'd been hit with a brick. Next thing, I'm on the floor.'

Dale nodded. His eyes flitted to her gut. The puddle was growing.

"You're a hero,' she said. 'Not many woulda done what you did."

The compliment off-sided Dale. It'd been a long time since he'd received one.

"What's your name?" he said.

"Polly. Yours?"

He told her.

"You got a kind face, Dale." She licked her lips, turning them ruddy. "You from round here?"

"Nah." He looked away. "Just passing."

"Where's home?"

"Shitsville."

"Where you headed next?"

"Haven't a clue."

She smiled again, said, 'Mystery man,' and her eyelids began drooping.

"Hey, Polly, don't fall asleep now!"

She blinked, refocusing. "Bit tired."

Keep her talking, Dale thought. 'How long you lived this way?"

"Twelve years. I work in the Co-Op. Got a little bungalow…" she stopped for breath. Exhaling, a hissing came from her chest. "It hurts."

"Polly!" Dale said. 'The ambulance is coming, love."

Was it? Were those sirens he heard? He couldn't tell.

"Bad luck, Dale," she said, "us getting caught up in this."

"Yeah, Polly."

"Is it cold?" Can't feel me legs."

He looked down at her body and wished he hadn't. The hole was gaping now, everything soaked in syrup. 'You're gonna be all right,' he whispered. 'I promise.'

He needed to apply pressure to stop the bleeding. Quickly, he pulled off his over-shirt, made a ball of it, placed it over the gunshot and pushed. Polly's face tightened.

"Easy,"he said.

In seconds, the shirt was soggy. She made that horrible hissing again. Then her right hand came up and rested on his. Their fingers intertwined.

"Maybe we'll go for a drink," she whispered.

"That'd be nice, Polly."

"You don't mind me asking?"

"Not at all." He followed her eyes.

She was looking at his arms. Dale's jailbird tats, normally hidden beneath his shirt, were now on full display.

"Where'd you get them?"

"Prison," he said.

"That man you shot, he's got ones like them on his arms."

"Yeah," Dale said. "He does."

"What you do to end up in there?"

'Made mistakes. Hurt people I loved.'

"I'm sure you never meant to."

Those were definitely sirens now, getting close.

"I'm sleepy, Dale…"

"Polly!" He heard his voice crack. "Stay, Polly!" He wanted to wipe his tears, but her hand wouldn't let go of his.

"You're still a hero to me…"

"We'll go for that drink, Polly! I'll pick you up from hospital. Polly? Polly!"

No more words.

Her lips parted for a final smile. Then her eyes closed and she died.

Dale stayed with her, cradling her head, stroking her hair. Time passed, just the two of them. Then it all fell apart.

"Armed police!"

Dimly, he looked up. Two rifles were aiming his way, held by a pair of fresh-faced coppers.

Behind them, shielded by police cars, was the newsagent man. He was wearing a flak-jacket, pointing at Dale accusingly.

"That's him! The second bastard robber! He shot the other lunatic and that poor woman too!"

"Armed police! Show your hands!"

But Dale didn't show his hands. Instead, he looked over his shoulder at the corpse of Mad Paddy, his old cellmate. Two days back, Paddy sprung up from nowhere offering Dale a 50-50 split for help with a newsagent holdup he promised couldn't go wrong.

"Just don't go psycho," Dale told his volatile acquaintance. "Promise?"

"Trust me," Paddy said with a wink.

Yeah, right.

Dale returned to the woman lying dead in his lap. She could've been sleeping.

"Sorry, Polly," he said. "Some hero." He reached behind for his bag.

The rifles flexed.

Inside, Dale found the cool steel Beretta. His finger touched its trigger. He grinned.

The gun was halfway out when the blasts tore through him. Dale fell straight back, one eye gone, the other staring at the same white sun Polly had been gazing at, until this, and everything, fizzled to blankness.

***

Still Life

Serena Jayne

With her life path paved with dodgy decisions, Kerry couldn't determine which of her many mistakes was to blame for her current situation. As a child, she'd dreamed of becoming an artist. Instead she used her keen eye for detail to build a small following as a forger. She prided herself on her ability to replicate signatures and legal documents. If not for her need for quick cash to replenish her supply of inks, paper, and holographic hoopla, she wouldn't be caught dead wearing a kooky cat costume and spinning a "Get Kitty Kat Kleen" sign on the corner of Loser and Nowhere.

Yet here she was, a living advertisement for car cleanliness, standing in front of the Kitty Kat Kleen carwash trying not to puke. The scratchy suit stank of weed, body odor, and rancid crab cakes from lack of laundering. Her pina colada body spray added a sickeningly sweet vomit-inducing dimension.

At the thought of her happy-go-lucky roommate donning the stupid suit six days a week without complaint, Kerry blinked back tears. Her brain broke down every detail of the tragic scene in their apartment into a still life—from Lou's inert body to the nearby syringe to the bag of smack with its odd symbol comprised of lines and a circle. The subject matter of a still life could involve any object as long as it's stationary. And the dead have a tendency to stay put.

Her roommate had been a hypervigilant addict, ever careful to use new needles, the smallest drug dose, and to only buy from trusted dealers. But nothing could protect Lou from a bad batch of junk.

Kerry had been working up the nerve to make an anonymous call to report Lou's death, when she'd come across his cat costume. Every Saturday at the end of his shift, he received the week's pay in cash from his Uncle Vince, the owner of Kitty Kat Kleen. Afterward, Lou would meet Kerry for mojitos, always insisting on paying for the first round. The tart, boozy drinks would forever remind her of Lou. And knowing him, he wouldn't want their mojito money to go unclaimed. It was practically her duty to put on the cat suit and play Lou long enough to collect the cash from his uncle.

His fleshy face flushed, Vince hurried past Kerry to enter the car wash office. The black canvas duffle bag hanging heavy on his shoulder contrasted with his tight salmon-colored t-shirt and sweatpants. Both items featured the carwash logo on their backsides.

Kerry stifled a giggle at the sight of the cartoon cat face stretched tight across Vince's saggy ass. The placement, which might work on a young gal with a perky posterior, became grotesque on the rear end of a doughy sixty-something dude.

*

Six sweaty hours later, the end of the shift finally arrived. Kerry's wrists and arms ached from swinging the sign, while her awful attire had taken its toll on her self-respect. At least she refrained from responding to the cat calls she'd received with obscene gestures.

She straightened her stance and added a jaunty spring to her step, imitating Lou's signature strut. With her hands covered in the fake fur of the

157

cat costume, turning the doorknob of Vince's small office was tricky. She stumbled inside and collided with his visitor.

The skinny dude kept his gun trained on Vince, but blinked his bloodshot eyes at Kerry. "Damn, Vince. You're one sick fuck. Figures you've got some twisted pussy cat fetish."

Lou's uncle grunted. "Nah, that's just my good-for-nothing nephew."

The guy with the gun returned his gaze to the car wash owner. "Well, I ain't leaving witnesses."

No way was Kerry going to meet her maker dressed like a cheap Hello Kitty knockoff. Her brain kicked into fight mode, and she whacked the skinny dude in the head with the sign.

The gun went off.

She kept fighting, using knees and elbows, and stomping him with her feet. All the emotion over the loss of Lou fed the fire. She was powerless to keep her friend from dying, but she could save his uncle.

When the thin man stilled, she kicked the gun away from his reach.

There was nothing zen or new agey about the new third eye between Vince's brows that the bullet had burned.

Bile rose in her throat, but she swallowed it back down.

She kicked the intruder again and nearly tripped over Vince's duffle. Unzipping the bag was awkward as hell, but she managed. Underneath the bricks of banded bills, she discovered dozens of small bags of smack marked with the symbol she now recognized as a crude depiction of a cat's nose and whiskers. A more simplistic version of the carwash logo and the same symbol from the bad batch of drugs that had killed her friend.

158

Kitty Kat Kleen had to be a front, making good old Uncle Vince responsible for Lou's death. If the bullet to the forehead hadn't done the job, Kerry would've killed him herself.

She gathered all the bags and dumped them on the desk, keeping the cash contained. Cash that would finance a fresh start whether she went the straight and narrow or continued to crave the crooked path. Cash that could weather her inevitable forthcoming sketchy decisions. Cash that would buy a shitload of mojitos in Lou's memory.

Kerry swore to keep syringes and smack out of the picture to avoid becoming a still life like Lou. She slid the strap of the duffle over her arm and, with as much dignity as someone wearing a cat costume could, stepped out into the world ready to forge a new future.

***

SWITCHBLADE
PERSON OF INTEREST

Name: Serena Jayne

Location: Illinois

First Appearance: Switchblade: Stiletto Heeled

Appearances: SB: Stiletto Heeled, SB Issues 10, 11, 12, 13

Although Serena Jayne has a longstanding love affair with all things paranormal, she's found a strong storytelling niche in crime fiction. Her short fiction has been featured in such notab] publications as *Crack the Spine Literary Magazine*, the *Oddville Press*, *UNRAVEL: A Crime Microfiction Anthology (Dark Drabbles Book 5)*, *The Monstrous Feminine: Dark Tales of Dangerous Women*, *LUST: The Shameful Vice of Impurity*, *Pulp Modern*, *The EconoClash Review*, and *Neon Druid*.

Switchblade had the oportunity to interview the indomitable Serena Jayne, who's appeared i more consecutive issues of SB then anyone else.

Who are you, where are you from, and how long have you been writing?

I'm a future-focused introvert with a number of obsessions. While I adore art, I have zero skill at translating my ideas into anything but eyesores. Writing in multiple fiction genres gives me the opportunity to grow a shiny story seed into something much closer to the vision that lurks inside my dark, cobweb-encrusted cranium.

I've always lived in the Midwest, having spent the majority of my years in Illinois, which I consider home. About ten years ago, I started seriously studying the craft of writing. In the process, I got to know many of my favorite authors on a personal level, which blows my mind. Reading short stories in no-holds-barred publications such as *Switchblade*

Magazine exposes me to cutting edge writing, which vastly improves my own work.

What makes a great story?

Great stories never fail to deliver a gut punch. They seem to contain a sliver of the author's soul. I love stories that go deep, take chances, and are unflinchingly crafted. For me, the best stories are ones that only the author could tell in their own particular way. Those stories tend to haunt me long after I've finished.

In life, every one of us is an unreliable narrator. We see the world through a narrow, cloudy, and sometimes cracked lens. Great stories contain characters who aren't simply good or bad, but somewhere in the gray, bleak middle ground.

Define noir.

Noir is often tragedy, full of less than heroic characters who are ruled by desperation and the impulsive id of the subconscious. Their focus is short term—survival in the immediate moment. Their future is tenuous. Each decision is steeped in moral ambiguity.

Why do you write in the noir genre?

Writing noir can be really cathartic. While dealing with a serious health issue last year, I channeled feelings of anger and powerlessness into a story called "Necessary Evils," which was published in *Pulp Modern*, volume 2, #5. The story is one of the meanest, nastiest things I've ever written. "Checking Out," which appears in *Switchblade* #12, involves the horror of pandemic grocery shopping. "The Nature of Nurture" in *Switchblade* #10 combines my obsession with games like Pokémon Go and thoughts of my ticking biological clock. I love exploring the darkness that skitters around in the world and inside of us all.

Who is the author who most influenced you?

Matt Andrew, author of crime and horror with stories in *Thuglit, Crime Syndicate Magazine,* and *Pantheon Magazine,* helped me refine my first noir story "Crazy Eights," which appeared in *Switchblade:*

Stiletto Heeled. He encouraged me to dig deeper and crammed my to-be-read list full of noir, introducing me to authors like Craig Clevenger, Will Christopher Baer, Denis Johnson, and Benjamin Whitmer. Matt directed me to movies and television series such as *Only God Forgives, Good Time, Blue Ruin, Too Old to Die Young,* and *Ozark.* If not for Matt's candor and encouragement, I wouldn't be the writer I am today. My fantastic critique partner Ara Hone gives me feedback on almost everything I write. She's a talented writer and editor, and I'd be lost without her tremendous support and friendship. Her beautiful writing can be found in *Pulp Modern Flash, Last Exit, Silver Blade Magazine, and Flash Fiction Magazine.* I'd be remiss if I didn't mention the kickass crime writing community on Twitter, and how much their support means to me. There, I got to know so many phenomenal people including C.W. Blackwell and Mark Pelletier. C.W. embodies the hustle, proving that writers can be prolific, while never failing to deliver an outstanding story. C.W.'s work can be found in *Switchblade Magazine, Pulp Modern, Rock and a Hard Place, EconoClash Review,* and *Mystery Weekly Magazine.* Mark, with his awesome #booktalk posts, lifts up the entire community of writers and readers by sharing his love of story.

Who is your favorite author in the independent crime fiction community?

Sarah Jilek is my favorite indie crime author. Her work is absolute fire and reminds me that while the jugular makes a great target, plenty of places bleed. Her characters are unapologetic and unforgettable. She brings back this combination of exhilaration and terror I felt as a kid, careening down a hill on my bike and realizing the brakes weren't working. I survived, but I was never quite the same afterward.

Sarah's just one of the amazing writers in *Switchbla Stiletto Heeled.* The issue also features Ann Aptaker Sarah M. Chen, Susan Cornford, Carmen Jaramillo, Sus Kuchinskas, Bethany Maines, Tawny Pike, Lissa Marie Redmond, Cindy Rosmus, Charlotte Platt, and E.F. Sweetman.

Lisa Douglass edited the volume and contributed a
wicked cool poem. I am damned proud to share a
table of contents with each author in *Switchblade
Magazine,* but there is a fierce and deadly beauty
unique to Stiletto Heeled.

SWITCHBLADE
Outlaw Apparel
wear a fucking mask!
NO
PANTS
REQUIRED
SWITCHBLADE
LOS ANGELES
EST. 2017
OUTLAW CULTURE
www.switchblademerch.com

ECONO CLASH review 6

Edited by
J.D. Graves

"Quality Cheap Thrills"

Time for your medicine.

Pulp Modern
Vol. 2 No. 6 — Summer 2020

Andrew Bourelle • "Doc" Clancy • Timothy Friend
Adam S. Furman • Nils Gilbertson • Peter W.J. Haye
Serena Jayne • Mandi Jourdan • Victoria Weisfel

CIRSOVA

A.B. PATTERSON

HARRY KENMARE, PI
AT YOUR SERVICE

PI Harry Kenmare loves gorgeous women, fine win
and Irish whiskey. And he loves to see justice don
He's old school: results matter, methods don't, ar
political correctness can go to hell, along with th
corrupt Establishment.

"*ake County Incidents* is like the Winesburg,
ˌio of the weird and wretched. Cizak's precise
ˌd simple prose proves the most horrifying
ˌng an author can show readers is a mirror."
ˌarc E. Fitch, author of *Paradise Burns*

MACABRE STORIES BY ALEC CIZAK

LAKE
COUNTY
INCIDENTS

ABC
ROUP DOCUMENTATION

Available
Now

INDIE RIGHTS

www.indierights.com

    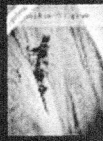  

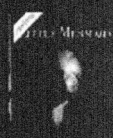      

Adventure

Action & Adventure

     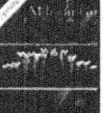 

      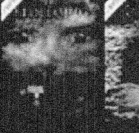

AN ANTHOLOGY OF NOIR

WITCHBLADE

WOMEN OF NOIR
SPECIAL ISSUE

NO LUCK TALES FROM SOME OF THE
MOST PROMINENT WOMEN IN CRIME FICTION

IT'S ALL WOMEN

IT'S ALL NOIR

IT'S ABOUT TIME

Author Bios & Acknowledgements

Brian Beatty is the author of the poetry collections "Dust and Stars: Miniatures" (2018, Cholla Needles Press), "Brazil, Indiana" (2017, Kelsay Books) and "Coyotes I Couldn't See" (2016, Red Bird Chapbooks). He lives in Saint Paul, Minnesota.

Serena Jayne received her MFA in Writing Popular Fiction from Seton Hill University. Before becoming a writer, she worked as a research scientist, a fish stick slinger, a chat wrangler, and a race horse narc. When she isn't trolling art museums for works that move her, she enjoys writing in multiple fiction genres. Her short fiction and poetry has appeared in *Switchblade Magazine, Crack the Spine Literary Magazine, the Oddville Press* and other publications. www.serenajayne.com

David Harry Moss has been published many times in print and online. Currently he lives in Pittsburgh but has also lived in Phoenix and Minneapolis. Other favorite haunts are New York City where he ran two marathons, Los Angeles where he frequented shrines like The Frolic Room, Clearwater Beach, Florida, and Paris, France

Stanton McCaffery's stories have been published in *Shotgun Honey, Out of the Gutter, Heater,* and *Yellow Mama.* His novel "Into the Ocean" is available from New Pulp Press. He is the Editor in Chief of *Rock and a Hard Place Magazine.*

David Rachels has published noir fiction in Switchblade, EconoClash Review, Mystery Tribune, and other similar places. As well, he has edited three volumes of Gil Brewer's short stories for Stark House Press.

Alec Cizak is a writer and filmmaker from Indiana. His books "Down on the Street", "Breaking Glass", and Lake County Incidents" are currently available from ABC Group Documentation. ABC will publish his latest novel, "Cool it Down", in 2021. He is also the editor of the fiction digest *Pulp Modern.*

Elliot F Sweeney is a crime writer from London. He's been published in *Switchblade* before, and has sold work to *Alfred Hitchcock, Suspense,* and others. Presently, he's working on a novel.

Danny Sophabmisay enjoys candlelit dinners, long walks on the beach, and writing about murderers, drug dealers, sex maniacs, and cats. He has stories in earlier issues of Switchblade.

Jay Rohr is a Chicago native with a taste for history, and wandering the city at odd hours. In order to deal with the more corrosive aspects of everyday life he writes the blog www.honestyisnotcontagious.com and makes music in the band Beerfinger. His Twitter babble can be found @Switch Blade

Robert Ragan A native of North Carolina, has had short fiction published online at *Vext Magazine, Punk Noir Magazine, Yellow Mama Webzine, Synchronized Chaos,* and *Terror House Magazine.* In January 2020, he had his second short story collection, "It's Only Art", published by Alien Buddha Press.

Andrew Bourelle is the author of the novel "Heavy Metal" and coauthor with James Patterson of *Texas Ranger and Texas Outlaw.* His short stories have appeared in *The Best American Mystery Stories, Mystery Tribune, Pulp Adventures, Pulp Modern, Thriller Magazine, Weirdbook Magazine*, and other journals and anthologies.

Gene Breaznell Twenty years ago, Gene Breaznell was hired off a tennis court by a guy who told him, "Forget this game, kid. I'll show you how to make money out of shit." The offer could not be refused. The job involved recycling in the New York City metro area, with a cast of characters worthy of The Sopranos. Breaznell is also the author of two hardcover mystery novels, and he has written for several national magazines.

George Garnet's fiction, has appeared or is forthcoming in a number of publications such as *Mystery Tribune, Switchblade, Out Of The Gutter, Mystery Weekly, The Dark City Crime and Mystery Magazine, The Literary Hatchet, Heater, eFiction Literary, Needle in the Hay, The Lady in the Loft, GKBC* and elsewhere. He lives in Melbourne down under.

Special Thanks to *The EconoClash Review*, Uncle B Publications, Mark Pelletier, and the Independent Fiction Alliance.